MASA

STORIES OF A LONE SOLDIER

ILAN BENJAMIN

MEISES BOOKS

Cover art and map design by Luke Patterson

Author illustration by Sarah Horwitz

ISBN-10: 0988435500
EAN-13: 9780988435506
Published by Meises Books
Library of Congress Control Number: 2012918631
CreateSpace Independent Publishing Platform
North Charleston, South Carolina

Dedicated to my Mother and Father
who had the courage to let me go.

MASA: Stories of a Lone Soldier
By Ilan Benjamin

Sheldon,

Thank you for your support!
This book would not be
possible without you!

Sincerely,

Ilan Benjamin

Meises Books

TABLE OF CONTENTS

INTRODUCTION

I was eight years old when I decided to join the Israel Defense Forces. I was a little boy on vacation with my family, sitting squished in between my big sisters in a grey minivan as it barreled down the Highway 90 in Israel.

On my knees were coloring books. In my hands were magic pens, the cool kind with the invisible ink. I was busy scribbling when I felt the minivan decelerate and then slow to an abrupt halt. Curious why my dad had stopped, I leaned forward past my sister to peer out the passenger window.

We were parked at the curb. A sign nearby read Gome Junction. I scanned the mountainous horizon and noticed a gas station and a couple of kibbutzim in the distance.

"Dad," I said, staring, "why did we—"

Then I saw him.

I saw him pick up a massive green bag, the same color as his clothes, and throw the strap of the gun—the gun!—over his left shoulder. The soldier approached the minivan, slid open the passenger door and smiled.

"Hi!" he said, looking around at the six of us. My dad asked him his destination. He replied. My dad told him to get into the car. So he did.

My sisters gathered together in the back seat, leaving him a space between the door and yours truly. All of our eyes were glued on the soldier, though I suspect what intrigued me and the girls differed greatly.

He put the bag below his seat and placed his black boots on top like one would an ottoman. He tucked a slip of his olive green shirt into his olive green pants, took his sunglasses off and readjusted the rifle so that the barrel reclined upon his right knee. All in one fluid motion.

1

Then he turned and looked at me and again he said, "Hi!"

I managed to mouth a greeting back. He asked me my name.

"Ilan," I said.

The soldier nodded and smiled and then turned to look toward the minivan's front window. I turned too. We watched the road peel back before us as my dad pressed his foot onto the gas pedal and took our family and the armed hitchhiker away.

He was the first Israeli soldier I ever met. He appeared to my eight-year-old self as the quintessence of cool and big and important.

Ten years later, I stood at a junction with my finger held out, wearing an olive green uniform and a gun strapped to my chest. A car pulled over, I smiled and I said, "Hi!"

This is the only non-fiction you will find in this book. *Masa* is a collection of short stories I wrote chronologically from before I enlisted in the Israel Defense Forces to afterward. Although the stories and the characters hold some stake in the real world, what mattered to me when I wrote, more than a literal retelling or a glorified diary, were emotional truths. Fiction allowed me to better tell the truth than fact.

The characters are all me and yet they are not. They are the what-ifs and the could-nots. They act upon yearnings that I was perhaps too cowardly or too brave to pursue myself; they are me at my best and my worst. And they are my friends, too, from Forward Platoon, Operations Company, Battalion 931, Nahal Infantry Brigade. They are every Israeli and American I ever met.

This is not a novel. I did not write it after the fact. I wrote these stories as they happened. The anger and betrayal you might feel reading "Abel" comes from the darkest hour of my service, my least hopeful moment, and I captured that moment by writing. The same goes for my happier stories.

The chronology of the book follows the four-year arc of my time in Israel. For the first year, I lived and volunteered on kibbutzim. Thus, "The Cheese War." A year later, I enlisted and began Basic Training on a base located in the middle of the Negev Desert, near the small city of Arad. Thus "The Mefaked." And so on and so forth.

After the "Masa," the grueling fifty kilometer hike for which this book is named, I graduated from advanced training and began to guard Israel's hottest borders: the West Bank, Lebanon and Syria, and the Gaza Strip.

I took the opportunity short fiction allows to experiment with different styles: first person and third, present tense and past. In some stories I paid homage to my favorite authors, such as "Aaron the Aryan," which I wrote a lá Damon Runyon. And two stories I chose to write as narrative poems.

It is a scrappy little book, an emotional rollercoaster. It is also the greatest single accomplishment of my life to date.

The eight-year-old boy in the grey minivan, gaping at the Israeli soldier—he is no different from the eighteen-year-old writer about to enlist in the Israel Defense Forces. Both the boy and the man fulfilled the famous words of Theodor Herzl.

"If you will it, it is no dream."

THE CHEESE WAR

It began innocently enough. A modest loaf of Brie de Meaux cheese slipped into the public fridge of the kibbutz volunteer dorm. The hands that both wrapped and then stored said dairy product belonged to one Jeanette Bouchard, a French native. Of course.

She bought the cheese for her fellow Frenchmen to enjoy together—a sentimental but overall harmless act. It reminded these new immigrants of the home they had left behind for Israel. Nobody could help themselves. The Americans downloaded *Grey's Anatomy* episodes, the Russian girl out-drank everybody, the Panamanians blasted house music so loud, their ears bled. Every person found a way to bring home into this foreign place.

But Jeanette's cheese was different from the television and the drinking and the music. Her act of nostalgia was different than all the others because it smelled. It smelled awful.

Had the stench of the well-matured brie been enclosed within the refrigerator, perhaps the following events would have played out differently. Such was not the case. The odor drifted from its cool confines into the nostril of every living habitant of the volunteer building, leaving its fetid scent in every crack and corner. No one could escape it.

The immediate reaction mirrored all previous melodrama. The cliques that had developed within this bizarre international congregation each shared their common outrage behind closed doors and turned backs. People were pissed but only to a verbal extent; they bitched and moaned with their compatriots. Everybody figured that eventually the scent would fade.

But three days later, the odor of the cheese remained strong. The Americans decided it was time to take matters into their own hands.

"Where is my cheese?!" screamed Jeanette. She had opened the fridge only to discover her moldy delicacy missing. Those present in the room averted their eyes and attempted to restrain the urge to laugh. One of these was Alonso Fontecilla, a Chilean tourist, whose grave mistake was to laugh a tad louder than the rest. One couldn't blame him. Jeanette noticed him snickering and used whatever twisted logic the enraged have to raise her arm and point.

"YOU!" she screamed.

His smile vanished as completely as the cheese.

"It wasn't me, Jeanette," he replied to the finger, nervous.

"NO?!" she asked.

He frowned and said, "...Yeah, no."

"Yeah or no?!"

"No, I mean no!"

Her bug-eyed gaze burned into his without mercy for the retinas.

"What did you do with my cheese, Alonso?" she asked, all snarl and menace. "I want it back!"

At that moment, one of the other onlookers, a Swiss kid, chose to inquire, "What's the big deal, Jeanette?" he asked. "It's just cheese, right?"

Had she had the time, it is possible that Jeanette would have explained to the Swiss how Louis XVI had asked for a taste of THIS cheese before he met the guillotine, how an international competition was won by THIS cheese in the Congress of Vienna and how, to this day in France, THIS cheese is considered the "King of Cheeses and Cheese of Kings".

Jeanette did not have the time for that so she told him to go back to "Switzerfuck" instead. When she turned back to glare at Alonso, he decided that he had heard enough.

"I didn't do anything, Jeanette," he said. "So leave me alone."

He walked off, leaving Jeanette alone to wallow in her rage and to contemplate revenge.

These events quickly became a yarn that spread and transformed, overwhelming the common boredom of the kibbutz volunteers with each telling. It was not long before one Erica Nelson heard the filtered gossip. She did her best to feign surprise at the news and then acceptance of its legitimacy, although she knew every word to be incorrect. This is because the night before she herself had extricated and then disposed of Jeanette's beloved cheese.

But Erica kept her mouth shut, afraid that if the French were aware of America's involvement, all hell would break loose. Only she and her British boyfriend, Ben, knew the truth. Meanwhile, Jeanette filled in her fellow Frenchmen (and two Canadians). When she had finished, they all agreed that an interrogation was in order.

Little did they know, their primary suspect had already assembled his own posse made up of fellow Spanish speakers, Avi the Bolivian, Estaven and Daniel the Panamafia, and Gavriel the Brazilian. Alonso had just finished recounting the tale to his allies, when the French arrived, fists pounding on his door. Estaven opened it.

"We need to talk to Alonso," said Nataniel, one of the French.

"He didn't take your cheese," Estaven said. "Ask somebody else."

"Then who did?"

"I don't know. I don't care."

Nataniel hesitated for a moment, eying Estaven.

"You know it is very expensive cheese?" Nataniel asked.

"Yeah," Estaven replied, "but it also smells horrible."

"So what?"

"So it smells everywhere because of your cheese."

"We don't complain about your shit music!"

And so the Kibbutz cold war got a whole lot hotter. Estaven, the muscle of the Spanish group, walked right up to Nataniel's face.

"You," Estaven said, "you've got five seconds to get the fuck out of my doorway."

Nateniel's jaw dropped two centimeters. He clenched it back into place and paused for two seconds, perhaps to reaffirm his testosterone level.

"Give us Alonso," he said.

Estaven grabbed Nataniel's shirt.

"I said, get out, you French fucking frog!"

A fist met Estaven's lower cheek and it began. The two little mobs pushed and kicked and bit their way in and out of the doorway like some morphing hourglass. Somebody's glasses flew off; they got crunched under the struggling feet. Other volunteers (Italians, Germans, Russians and a South African) rushed over in an attempt to calm down both sides. A few stray punches came their way; peace treaties were forgotten. They joined in the mayhem.

It grew louder and bloodier and uglier. The Swiss kid, walked up and asked, "What are you all fighting about?"

Avi the Bolivian grabbed his shirt in fistfuls and chucked him. A second later, they all heard a huge crash and creaking, the sound of wood splintering. Everybody stopped to look, fists frozen in midair. This Swiss sat in the remains of a cupboard. They stared at the wooden corpse and then dispersed without another word. They scrambled back to their rooms as if nothing had ever happened.

Alonso managed to come out of the chaos unscathed. Shaking his head, he collapsed onto his bed and sighed. Then he sat up. Somebody had knocked on his door. He opened it cautiously this time, afraid his room might again become ground zero, but it was just Ben, the British fellow.

"What's up Ben?" Alonso asked.

"Not much," Ben replied, "Mind if I come in?"

Ben did not wait for a response. He walked in and closed the door and then stared intently at Alonso.

"I'm telling you this in confidence, Alonso," he said, voice full of portentous foreboding. "I don't want you to get hurt."

"What do you mean?" Alonso asked.

Ben sighed, "I know you didn't take Jeanette's cheese."

"Well, of course—"

"No, I know because...I know who did it."

Alonso's eyebrows arched up.

"And you're telling me this now?" he asked.

"I know," Ben said. "I'm sorry. I just don't want her to get in trouble."

"Her?"

He needn't have asked. Suddenly Alonso understood the whole ghastly scheme.

"Erica?"

Ben nodded. Alonso shook his head.

"You fucking Americans," he said.

"I'm not American," Ben said.

"You're all the same."

"You can't tell Jeanette. She'll kill her!"

Alonso shook his head. He knew what he ought to do—mosey over to Jeanette's room and tell her the truth. But no, Alonso did not fancy himself a rat. He would take the fall for the cheese. He would spare the American princess and her cuckold British boyfriend. He decided, not out of some misplaced sense of martyrdom, but because, after all was said and done, he really had enjoyed pissing off Jeanette and those French sons of bitches. He looked back at Ben.

"I was going to steal the cheese anyways," Alonso admitted. "It smelled like shit."

AARON THE ARYAN

Today, the nerves of Aaron the Aryan are strung higher than the laundry on his ever-loving mother's clothesline and, as you likely know, the ever-loving mother of Aaron the Aryan lives in a very tall building indeed.

Now, the source of this young man's sudden bout of anxiety is a tad too byzantine to illustrate sans some knowledge of yesteryear. So I figure that the most commonsensical thing to do is to retreat back to before Aaron the Aryan is known as Aaron the Aryan and just called little Aaron Klotsky. This way, you may better understand how he eventually becomes so nervous and such.

No knock to Aaron the Aryan intended, but he grows up without much of a clue in the world, living so charmed and bubbled an existence in a little town by the name of La Jolla. He is born here on one humdrum day, sporting blond hair and royal blue eyes, neither of which bears much of a resemblance to the features of his ever-loving parents. The only thing he is sharing with them in fact is a very fair epidermis, which does not remain that way for very long once he begins sun-bathing so much.

Soon after, little Aaron Klotsky learns to walk, talk, and surf as good as anybody. And eventually it becomes rather difficult to discern between him and any other flip flop-clad La Jollan. Except, little Aaron Klotsky is different, you see. It turns out that Aaron Klotsky is really very Jewish.

So Jewish in fact is little Aaron Klotsky that it is a challenge to find even a twig of gentile on the deftly-researched Klotsky family tree. Mister and Missus Klotsky are of course very pleased to admit this and crow about it often at parties and galas and potlucks and such. But I wish to say

I never find being very Jewish so impressive, personally, because I am never understanding what makes one more or less so, and furthermore, being an atheist, I don't see the attraction to being very religion-oriented anyway.

Well, by and by little Aaron Klotsky becomes not so little and gets to wondering more than somewhat about his Jewish forebears. One day he asks his ever-loving mother, "Where are we from before La Jolla?" Now, Missus Klotsky is happy to tell this not-so-little Aaron Klotsky that once upon a time they spring from a land flowing with bees and dairy products, but she hesitates.

Wonders she, "Why tell my not-so-little son, when I can show him?"

Indeed, Missus Klotsky becomes so enamored with the idea that she forgets to answer the question of Aaron Klotsky in the first place. Off she runs to convince Mister Klotsky that they must visit the place of -ites and -isms, and he is similarly smitten by the notion. And so it happens that Aaron Klotsky and the Mister and Missus end up on sitting on an aeroplane aimed square for the so-called Holy Land.

To abridge a few dull as dishwater chapters, let us just say that when Aaron Klotsky sees his homeland for the first time, he acts very daffy indeed. And his ever-loving parents turn out to be quite partial to remaining yonder for some time as well. Personally, I will have to be paid more than somewhat to habitate in such a sandy place, but the Klotskys appear to relish the environment no little. I might add that scratch is no issue when you are as well-heeled as a Klotsky.

Anyway, some time passes and Aaron Klotsky turns eighteen years of age. And it is on this birthday that he discovers, much to his La Jollan dismay, that he must serve in the so-called Holy Land's Israelite military and any minute now at that.

Meanwhile, I happen to be vacationing in the so-called Holy Land myself and am sitting with Uzi Izzy in Phedinkus, a little joint on the south side of Dizengoff Street one Sunday morning at about four o'clock, finishing my drink all quiet like, when who barges in more daffy than a bull seeing red but Aaron Klotsky.

Of course, this causes great indignation among the other customers trying to enjoy their hangovers in peace and quiet, but Aaron Klotsky, who is worried stiffer than a bad case of rigormortis, does not seem to notice. He drops into a chair alongside Uzi Izzy, and then orders a kubbe-duo with sliced onions to come along, which is a dish that is considered most invigorating, and immediately Aaron Klotsky begins telling of his woes, although nobody asks him to. So Aaron Klotsky tells us as follows:

Well, (Aaron Klotsky says) according to Hershel the Heckler, all citizens of the so-called Holy Land must do some sort of military service and this includes myself. Now, at first I consider this earful nothing more than phonus bolonus and furthermore I hold little confidence in the word of a shifty type like Hershel the Heckler. So, I ask Gadi Shimon, who is seldom misinformed, for his two cents worth. But I forget that Gadi Shimon speaks little to no English, and so he starts frowning and raising his eyebrows more than somewhat until I remember.

Well, what happens but right at that moment my ever-loving mother is walking by, mittens full of groceries and what not. I figure she might know a thing or two about this military business, so I stop her and say:

"Ma! Wait a minute! Do you have any idea what is with this military business?"

"Why," my ever-loving mother says, "do you not hear? Mr. Klotsky receives your conscription form in the mail today!"

Now of course all this is surprising news to me, indeed, (Aaron Klotsky says) and in fact I am quite flabbergasted, and as for understanding it, all I understand is that I'm getting a rotten deal and that frankly I will never come to the so-called Holy Land in the first place if I know I must serve in the Israelite military.

"Well, Aaron," I say after hearing all this, "it is a very unfortunate story and full of shocks and this and that, and," I say, "of course I will never be so inconsiderate to call a guy a sap, but," I say, "if it is not naive to move to a country before reading the fine print, then it will do until something more naive comes along."

Well, this is not cheering up Aaron Klotsky so much and I figure his case is just about hopeless when Uzi Izzy suddenly perks up.

"What makes you so sure you are eligible?" Uzi Izzy asks Aaron Klotsky.

"What do you mean?" Aaron replies.

"Well, unless you are very certainly certified Jewish," says Uzi Izzy, "to my knowledge, you are not forced to serve."

Aaron Klotsky considers this for a second but then continues to sulk. "I'm afraid I am very certainly certified Jewish." he says, "In fact, I believe there are few people as certainly certified Jewish as me."

Upon hearing this, Uzi Izzy is looking very forlorn indeed, and I wish to say I see many a drooping kisser in my life, but I never see one so sad as Uzi Izzy's in that moment. And all three of us are quiet for some time, which is considered customary in such cases. But then, while giving Aaron Klotsky a worried gander, a thought suddenly crosses my mind.

"Why, Aaron," I say, "you don't *look* so Jewish."

"No?" he asks.

"In fact, if I am never meeting you, I will say you resemble just about anything but Jewish."

"I guess I do!" he exclaims and chances are we both guess right.

Then Uzi Izzy gives Aaron Klotsky a quick once-over too and asks: "How do you become so gentile-like anyway, Aaron?"

"Well, I am born and raised in La Jolla, you see," Aaron Klotsky says, "and if one lives in La Jolla, there is little choice regarding one's genetics."

Now this of course is making no sense but I have not the heart to tell Aaron Klotsky so, and furthermore I don't wish to burst some newly sanguine bubbles regarding Aaron Klotsky's draft-dodging prospects.

Anyway Uzi Izzy, Aaron Klotsky, and I begin to form a plan so as to convince the Israelite military that Aaron Klotsky is really just as non-Jewish as he resembles. And by and by, this is how Aaron Klotsky gets to being called Aaron the Aryan.

Now if you are never having to partake in something by the name of Tzav Rishon, I wish to say you miss nothing much because what is it but a room full of very testy testosterone at work. There are plenty of almost-military men taking tests from already-military men all on behalf of this so-called Holy Land's military and it is a very sore sight indeed.

And it happens to be on this day and spot that Aaron the Aryan finds himself in that prior mentioned state of tremendous anxiety. Today, you see, is his one opportunity to convince the Israelite military that he is not belonging in an Israelite military in the first place and he is sweating plenty of bullets over the matter. Aaron the Aryan sits awhile all on his lonesome, picking his knuckles into a ghastly state as young people are liable to do, when at last a little man bustles in to the room.

He is a pretty wide guy, very heavy set, and slow moving, and with jowls that you can slice shawarma off of, and tired run-down eyes, and he somehow resembles an old basset hound that just happens to be in military uniform. Walking around the desk, he takes a seat across from Aaron the Aryan, glances at him and then starts to chatter-train in his native tongue.

Now of course Aaron the Aryan is not in a position to interrupt the wide induction officer, because he figures he is liable to hurt his fair-shake at cajolery. Anyway, he does not wish to make this wide induction officer mad, as he is apt to strong-arm Aaron the Aryan into an undesirable unit in some awfully sandy place if so he wishes.

So, Aaron the Aryan does not request a translation and just sits there, nodding his head every couple of seconds at the wide induction officer as he twaddles of this and that. Then after a few minutes, the wide induction officer opens his desk drawer and pulls out a piece of paper and a pen and slides it toward Aaron the Aryan matter-of-factly, chatting all awhile. But Aaron the Aryan is not letting a single finger linger on the paper, being very weary of signing sheets that he does not understand and such.

So eventually the wide induction officer notices this and stops to look at Aaron the Aryan curiously. Then he says, "You don't *look* very Jewish."

Well, Aaron the Aryan is very gratified indeed that the wide induction officer at last stops chattering away, and is about to compliment the man's gentile-radar, when the wide induction officer interrupts: "But your file seems to suggest that you are so."

"My file?" he asks.

"Yes, yes. Everybody has a file, you see. And according to yours, the Klotsky family tree is well populated with very Jewish figures."

Panicking, Aaron the Aryan starts, "But the thing is, I am not Jewish."

"No?"

"No, not even a smidgen."

The wide induction officer takes a good long meddling gander at Aaron the Aryan for a few moments before turning to stuff his head into a bunch of paperwork. Aaron the Aryan, meanwhile, feels more than somewhat uneasy, certain that he is playing all his cards and that the jig is about to be up. And just when he considers coming clean with the honest truth, the wide induction officer pulls his head out of the plentiful folders and papers and whatnot, and interrupts Aaron the Aryan once again.

"It appears you are right!" he says.

Well, naturally Aaron the Aryan is very much surprised at this statement, because he is not right, and he is Jewish as a matter of fact, and if the file claims the contrary then this is a very peculiar circumstance indeed.

"How do you figure?" Aaron the Aryan asks.

"Why," the wide induction officer responds, "Do you not know? You are adopted after turning two years of age and your real family tree is not certainly certified Jewish in the slightest. In fact, there's not even a twig of Jewish in sight!"

Now as it turns out, Aaron the Aryan is in fact an Aryan with not a Jewish bone in his bodice and when he confronts his ever-loving parents on the matter, they tell him an astonishing story indeed. Apparently, Mister and Missus Klotsky are always wanting to tell little Aaron Klotsky that he is not an honest Klotsky, but they never get around to it. And furthermore, when they decide to live in the so-called Holy Land, they figure that by and by Aaron won't mind serving in the Israelite military, being so daffy about the spot and all. But personally, I know this cannot be true, for if there is one thing a non-Jewish La Jollan never yearns for, it is to serve in an Israelite military.

Anyway, Aaron the Aryan resolves to mull over all these revelations and I hear he is taking a flight straight back to La Jolla to meet his real ever-loving parents just the next day. So this is about all there is to the story, except that when Aaron the Aryan decides to return to the so-called Holy Land and forgive the ever-loving Klotskys for misleading him and keep being Jewish anyway, he ends up volunteering in the Israelite military while he's at it. And last I hear, they still call him Aaron the Aryan in there on account of his very La Jollan looks.

THE MEFAKED

They too have souls. They too have mothers and girlfriends and homes to return to, childhood friends to commiserate with on every petty injustice and betrayal they have endured. They too daydream in the desert of a nourishing meal and of more than five minutes to eat it. They sweat, they drink Coke, they laugh and they talk shit. They check Facebook and reminisce on all the drunken debauchery they enjoyed back in high school.

Sometimes they see the same mirages of civilization, of proof that there is life outside this army and don't know whether to laugh or cry when the vision inevitably dissolves into dust. And of course, they too once were *tzairim*, a Hebrew word—part endearing, more insulting—used for the Israeli army's newcomers. Yes, even the *mefakedim*, the commanders, were once tzairim. Like me.

But right now, that all seems too hard to believe.

"KEEP CRAWLING!" Mefaked Doron Levi bellows, veins pulsing violently out of his neck like weaving flashfloods in the desert. He lets out his most head-splitting shriek yet.

"WAKE UP! You weak pieces of shit, you jokes!!! What do you think this is? Summer camp? A hiking trip? Crawl faster now or I will stick my arm so far up your–"

You get the point. I'm smack dab in the middle of Basic Training and right now all I want to do is kill my *mefaked*. He's a short guy, probably a chain smoker, with a face only a mother could love (with difficulty). His perpetually scrunched, sun-blotched expression dominated by a long

crooked crease between his eyebrows makes him very, very easy to imper-
sonate. This we all do with glee.

Especially easy to parrot is his trademark, impossible-to-obey command: "SHUT YOUR FACE!" He squawks the line at least three or four
times a day, spittle flying from his mouth with such impressive velocity, it
is difficult to keep said shut face straight.

In order to stay sane and not commit homicide, we laugh...usually
at Mefaked Doron. We tend to joke behind his back from a safe distance
away. But, no, not today. As I lie in the wilderness, frying under the un-
forgiving Middle Eastern sun, getting berated for not bloodying my elbows
enough, it happens. I crack.

"Crawl!" Mefaked Doron orders.

I thrust the M-16 forward and kick my boots against sand in search of
traction. I push on, my vest sagging along the desert floor.

"FARTHER!" he screams.

My knee-pads slide down my legs, impotent. Jagged rocks and splinters
pierce the skin on my knees.

"FASTER!"

The back of his foot meets my ass, sending me airborne. A second
later, I face-plant right into an ant-hill. Dirt and sand and insects fly up my
nostrils, making me cough, sneeze, spit. I am amused no longer.

No, now I'm rage incarnate. As the mefaked moves on to other victims,
I begin to feel insane and invincible – ready to withstand whatever creative
hell he's got hidden up his sleeve. Make me run, crawl, do a couple hundred pushups – whatever strikes your fancy, you sadistic fuck! It's worth
any and every punishment just to make you look like a complete idiot for
the next couple of seconds.

I stand up and I wait. It takes Mefaked Doron a few seconds to notice;
he's too busy grabbing my friend Yoav by the collar and dragging him.

But when he finishes with Yoav and sees me standing there, he throws his reflexive tantrum.

"Jeremy!" he yells. "What do you think you're doing?! Drop! Get back down and crawl! Don't make me—"

Before he can finish, before I have a chance to second-guess the possible consequences, I do it. Face scrunched into an ugly scowl, voice lowered to a trembling overdone bravado, finger pointed centimeters away from his nose, I scream.

"SHUT YOUR FACE!"

Silence. His jaw drops – quite literally, as if about to ingest a massive deli sandwich. The soldiers stop crawling. They stare in awe at my outstretched arm, my posture. This imitation they have all seen and more than half of them done themselves before. But always behind Mefaked Doron's back. Not to his face.

This is real, uncut 100% chutzpah and lord, are they scared for me. It feels like a whole eternity has passed; no one dares to move, stuck in the strangest still-life ever painted. Then without warning, something remarkable happens. Mefaked Doron laughs.

I don't know at first if this is really happening. I am certain I am dead or hallucinating because there is no possible way that in this life or any other, my mefaked could have the capacity to laugh. But he's still at it. He shakes his head with self-deprecating glee, giggles as if he were physically tickled, an irresistible grin spread across his face.

And now everyone laughs and some people laugh so hard they cry. The soldiers, still lying on the ground, begin to howl. Their hands slap the sand, sending it skyward. They roll around as if they've never seen or heard something so hilarious. I'm going along with them, half-shocked, half-jubilant.

Most of all, I'm relieved that I remain alive and that it turns out Mefaked Doron has a sense of humor. For even though his job is to be the biggest bastard in the world, to turn us tzairim into real soldiers and to break us in order to do so, Mefaked Doron is only human, funny bone included.

Eventually we all calm down and the mefaked calls me over to the side. I know that whatever is coming can't be good, that such a gracious moment can only be short-lived, so I approach him cautiously. He waits for a moment, still smiling, and then puts his hand on my shoulder.

"You know, Jeremy," he says, "we mefakedim make fun of you guys too."

I nod, a bit surprised. I try to imagine him imitating us. This is still too big a stretch.

"Now, I have to punish you, of course," Mefaked Doron says. "This is clear. But I wanted to remind you that I was once in the exact same spot you are now. Don't worry; Basic Training will end soon. When it's over, we can laugh together again."

He shoots me one last grin, a real sincere one, and I'm struck by how misguided my prejudices seemed. He's really not that ugly after all. In fact, he acts like a pretty decent guy in real life. Maybe if I think of him as Doron Levi, maybe if I remind myself that he's not always a mefaked, then I will get through Basic Training just fine. I don't think I even want to kill him anymore.

A few minutes later, I take that back.

ABEL

Abel was the sort of guy you couldn't call a son of a bitch without feeling sorry for his mother. She already had it bad enough having born him.

Loud, massive, and about as sharp as a snooker ball, Abel might have been a fine fit in the U.S. Marine Corps. Alas, he joined our army—the Israeli one—instead and for two months of Basic Training graced us with his offensive presence. We hated him long before the morning he decided to blow his dumb American brains out in the platoon's only working bathroom stall but even more so afterward. Abel, as if thumbing his nose at us one last time, left behind a hell of a mess.

'Twas my fortune to be on cleaning duty that day and thus find myself face to face, so to speak, with the rancid remains of Abel. I came prepared for the shit and the blood. I did not come prepared for the brains. Pink as the goddamn panther cartoon, they were scattered all over the place. Maybe I should have held it against the military police for their lack of precision in body collection or begrudged the mefaked for ordering me to do the dirty deed, but…no. I just blamed Abel.

Beginning to scrape some of his congealed jelly off the toilet handle with the backside of a sponge, I admit that my outrage subsided. Eventually. In its place emerged a pensive mood. This substance, I thought, was only a few hours ago the upper story of a man—not a particularly large or inspired one, but a working brain nonetheless. One bullet later, it'd been reduced to soup. Crazy. And, waxing rather sentimental, I considered my first memory of the remains I was mopping up.

21

"I DON'T UNDERSTAND YOU!" screamed the American man-child. "WHAT DO YOU WANT FROM ME?!"

Licking some leftover couscous he had discovered in the corner of his mouth, the one they called Abel rose to his full height and flailed his flabby arms about like two scared chickens. There in that muddy, dimly-lit mess hall, he seemed, next to his mefaked, a boulder aside a pebble. Let it be known that as much as I loathed this ash-colored slob of a mefaked, I wouldn't have wished Abel on my worst enemy. He was harebrained chaos incarnate. And did I forget to mention? The kid couldn't even speak a word of Hebrew.

"You--you cannot eat yet," the mefaked tried in English.

"WHY NOT?!" Abel belched.

"It is forbidden to eat now."

"SO WHEN CAN I FUCKING EAT?!"

"When I give permission."

"GIVE WHAT? I DON'T UNDERSTAND YOU!"

"Permission."

"WHAT THE FUCK IS PEHMEESHEN?!"

"Per-Mish-Un!" shouted the mefaked.

"WHAT ABOUT IT?!" shouted back Abel.

"You cannot eat without my permission. Stop eating!"

"Oh," said Abel. "You could've said so from the start."

Abel sat back down. He clutched his fork and knife in sweaty fists, waiting about as patiently as a Tel Aviv taxi driver in Friday traffic. The mefaked, frozen on the spot, just stared at this expletive-spewing behemoth in horror. We all—we sad, sane Israelis forced by law to enlist—took a good long gander at Abel, at a person who had volunteered to enlist in a country's army he had nothing to do with, and together we wondered: *What the hell is this American doing here?*

To be fair, there were some other lone soldiers around who were actually bearable, like Jeremy Berman or Aaron Klotsky. To be less fair, even the nice ones were brainwashed suckers. No human being in their right mind would come join this godforsaken army unless spoon-fed ancient half-truths about the good ol' glory days of the IDF. And even then, most of these idealistic Zionists would be wise enough to keep their love at an arm's length—say, from some college's Hillel event. No, the truth is that these lone soldiers were either losers or crazies. As for Abel? He fit snugly into both categories.

They claimed that their connection to Israel was beyond words, an inexplicable link between land and man, and an embodiment of their ancestry and blah blah bullshit. At least Abel was (allegedly) honest. When asked, like all the other lone soldiers were asked, why he decided to immigrate and join the army, Abel said, "I want to kill some sand-niggers."

We said, "You could have just joined the American army to do that."

He replied, "No Palestinians in Iraq."

For a while, the source of Abel's hatred, for it was a hatred more sincere than any I have ever encountered, remained a mystery. Did he have friends or family who'd been blown up by suicide bombers? No. Did he maybe have an Israeli uncle or cousin who'd died by the hand of Hamas? He did not. But it was personal. It had to be. Abel did not merely loathe the terrorists, you see. He loathed them all.

Others felt the same, but others had their reasons. Abel's rage was senseless. My best attempts to psychoanalyze him proved fruitless. All potential answers he muddled with his furious idiocy.

"Abel," I asked him in the first week of basic training, "why do you hate them so much?"

"Who?" he asked.

"Arabs."

"Cause they're stupid Arabs," he said.

"Okay," I said, speaking slowly, "but why?"

"I don't understand you," said Abel.

"Maybe you just need something to hate?"

"I don't understand you," said Abel.

"What I'm saying is—do you hate Arabs because you're looking for something to hate and they just happen to fit the bill?"

"You speak English like a retard," said Abel. "I don't understand anything you're saying."

From then on out, I gave up giving a shit.

Of our few remaining conversations, none ever led me to believe that Abel would self-destruct someday. Then again, to talk to Abel was to resist throttling the kid by his fat gullet. None of us ever paid much attention to what he actually had to say. Why? Because a conversation with Abel usually consisted of racist tangents or unwarranted sex threats or early 90's "your mama" jokes.

Usually. But I do remember one night when Abel spoke as if he were a normal person, one filled with pain and dignity and even a little whimsy. Late one night, believing that we'd all fallen asleep, Abel spoke into a cell phone.

"Yeah," he said. "Yeah. No. No. I don't know."

I did not understand at first. I thought he must be talking in his sleep, which is when he mentioned her.

"It's okay, Mom," Abel said. "I'm happy. Everyone really likes me and they think I'm funny."

He stopped. She must have been talking.

"No, I get their language really easy…Yeah. I miss you too."

He stopped again. Silence. Then he said: "Don't worry. I'm gonna find him, Mom."

He was quiet. I thought the conversation might continue but it never did and eventually the hush took me with it into the confines of slumber. When I woke, I believed it a dream and nothing more.

They called it Abel-sitting. One month into basic, driven so crazy by Abel, the mefakdim devised a rotation. Each day, one mefaked had to personally accompany Abel everywhere, attempting to keep him out of trouble. Whether this meant preventing Abel from assaulting a shooting instructor who had dared criticize his prowess with an M-16 or saving the life of an army cook who'd had the gall to make Abel clean a dish, the mefakdim had their work cut out for them. But one day, on the ashy-looking mefaked's day to be precise, Abel managed to ditch his guard. Fifteen minutes later they found Abel behind a dumpster, strangling a stray cat.

For that, Abel got two weeks on base without leave. But this did not rectify or rehabilitate Abel. On the contrary, all that time in one place just made him wilder. It was as if the hounds of hell had been lying dormant until now. First, Abel robbed the canteen. He then proceeded to piss in a fellow soldier's Camelbak. Disappointed by the rather timid reaction these acts received, Abel became acquainted with the brigade's visiting Lieutenant-General by walking up to the balding 68-year-old war hero and head-butting him. When the lieutenant-general had recovered from his mild concussion, he demanded that Abel be punished.

Abel got a month on base without leave. No more.

In any reasonable army, a guy like Abel would not have gotten away with such mischief. Then again, were this a reasonable army, Abel would never have made it past the paperwork on induction day. The IDF, you must understand, has about as much bureaucratic commonsense as an Arab country's democratic process. So, it's no surprise that a guy like Abel slipped through the cracks into combat. I've heard rumors that he lied to

25

the induction officers regarding his history of mental illness, physical capabilities, and prior arrests in order to get in…all of which I find hard to believe. This seems far too clever a move for Abel.

More likely is that he told the truth and no one gave two uniformed shits. Considering how desperate this country is to fill its lacking infantry, they would have taken a guy like Abel no matter how dumb, crazy or downright evil he ended up. This, I assume, is how Abel got thrown into combat training and why, when he turned out to be mentally deranged, they refused to kick him out. He could pull any prank, break any rule, decline any command; it made no difference. Abel was stuck. Because the country needed its warriors. And country comes first. Hoorah.

Then one day everything changed. We woke up to find *jobniks* everywhere, filling out forms, interviewing soldiers in regards to their status and special needs. In other words, the jobniks came to update the rather vague files we filled out on induction day. I was standing in a line, which is to say, in a massive pile of punching elbows and sweaty curses, as is the custom in my country in regards to waiting, when I heard an inhuman shriek.

"YOU LYING TWATTEL!"

Abel was responsible for the holdup. I lifted my head above the throng of lurching bodies to take a look at what had enraged the American this time and was taken aback. Abel appeared less fuming than he did…afraid. He sat across from an impatient jobnik girl. She held his paperwork in her hand as if they were his balls.

"I said," she said, "that your citizenship status was written wrong. You have a parent living in the country, which means you are not a lone soldier but a returning citizen and—"

"I don't understand you!" Abel shouted. "Speak clear!"

"Your father—he lives in Israel?"

"In Palestine."

"You mean Israel."

"I mean Palestine."

"There is no such thing."

"I don't understand you."

"Look," she said, exasperated, "I don't know what the misunderstanding here is all about. Take this paper. It has the correct contact information and address of your father."

She handed him a paper. Abel took it, looking dumbfounded. It was the first time I'd seen the expression on his face. Most comments, insults, and laughter tended to bounce off of him as if he were immune to the world's judgments, unaware of the reality around him. I had never seen him react to anything but a command. Until now.

Abel ran off without another word. A few minutes later we could hear, even from a considerable distance, the guy going berserk. I pulled myself out from the clump of people and darted over to see what was happening. Abel stood towering over his grey mefaked once again. He breathed heavier than a racehorse, he sweated bucket loads and he clutched the paper in his chubby hands.

"LET ME OUT!" Abel shrieked.

"Abel," the mefaked began, "you don't remember? You were given a punishment."

"Fuck the punishment! I need to go!"

"You can't go. You have to stay another two weeks on base."

"If you don't let me go—"

"What, Abel?" the mefaked asked, suddenly defiant. "Are you going to hit me? Kick me? Go ahead if you want more weeks."

Abel looked at the mefaked. He seemed to be trying to understand the man's logic.

"Wait," Abel said. "If I hit you and kick you, you will do what?"

"Make you stay here longer."

"You don't understand! I need to go today. Right now."

"No, you don't understand, Abel. You aren't going anywhere."

Abel hesitated, likely in attempt to do the math. He then proceeded to hit and kick the mefaked with great vehemence. It took four or five soldiers to pull him off. When they'd succeeded, the mefaked was hospitalized immediately and, as for Abel—he received another two months on base. This order he respected as much as he respected any order. On that same day Abel left the base on foot, hitchhiked to the closest bus stop, and left. He was classified, by all official standards, AWOL.

For a while it was as if he'd vanished. Then two weeks later, the grapevine let out that military police had found Abel and thrown him into prison. Apparently, he would be back on base in a few days. Nobody took this news well. The most peaceful period of our army service, we believed, would end abruptly with Abel's arrival.

How wrong we were.

Abel returned a different man. Still fat, still stupid, still as unpleasant as ever, but no longer so audible with these traits. He'd been silenced. Most people assumed that jail had done it to him. But I knew better. From all I'd heard of military prison, it sounded downright cozy compared to base. I guessed it had to do with that paper he'd been ranting about, something to do with his father. But truth be told, I couldn't care less. I was just glad that something had shut the dumb American up.

Soon after, Abel requested to be dishonorably discharged. They denied it. Abel requested a shortened service. Denied again. Finally, he asked for his one-month vacation in the States—a right every lone soldier is entitled to—and they told him, "No." He still had half a year of punishments to fulfill before he could go anywhere. Abel requested no more.

Then one morning, this morning, Abel went "blam!" and ceased to exist. I'd almost finished cleaning, almost erased any trace that a guy's noggin had been sprayed all over just a few minutes ago like a feature at a modern art gallery, when I saw it. Scrawled on the bathroom stall's door in sharpie, amongst a series of graffiti and quotes and dick jokes, were three words freshly scribbled: Abel's last words.

He'd tried his best to write them in Hebrew, which I found oddly honorable, as if with his last breath he'd felt some urge to be one of us, to be a fellow Israeli. But he'd fucked it up. Abel had meant to write: "היה פה אבל" or: "Abel was here". What Abel wrote however was: "אבל היה פח" or: "Abel was trashcan."

Attendance was not mandatory but most of us came to the funeral anyway. It meant getting away from base, out of the desert, and into civilization. All pluses. I could suffer the one minus: having to feign sympathy for a dead asshole. The army really pulled out the stops this time. Abel got a military service, all formalities and niceties included, at Har Herzl, the graveyard where countless Israeli heroes have been laid to rest over the years. I imagined a montage of names: *Meir...Netanyahu... Senesh...Abel.*

After a series of speeches by different lieutenants and colonels regarding the "tragedy," remembering this lone soldier's "courage," and so on an so forth in a rather transparent attempt to cover their asses for Abel's dead one, I began to reconsider my decision. What was worse? Listening to all this talk of martyrdom and misfortune over a guy everybody agreed was better off dead or being on base? A tough choice.

Then a woman stood up in whose face I read new wrinkles and in whose eyes I recognized those of another. Abel's mother approached the microphone, stood in front of it statue-still and then spoke in clear English.

"My son was a bastard," she said.

I couldn't help it. I grinned bigger than the Cheshire Cat.

"My son was a bastard because he was fatherless," she said, correcting my amused train of thought.

"The man you might call his father left us when Abel was five. He did not call. He did not write. He did not care about me or Abel or anything but his new life in Israel. He remarried and had, from what I hear, three adorable children. But I never told Abel any of that. I refused to tell him anything. And that's the way it was, like a family secret. But when Abel turned sixteen, he wanted to know the truth."

Abel's mother began fidgeting with her hands, squeezing and pulling the skin on her knuckles.

"I did try," she said, "but I was so scared that the truth would break my sensitive boy in half. I needed a better story—something inspiring. This was all around the time Gilad Shalit had been kidnapped and it was all over the news and fresh in my mind and...anyway, it was the best explanation I could come up with. I told Abel that his father was an Israeli war hero being held captive by Palestinian terrorists."

I turned to my left, then to my right, and saw that every soldier's face wore the same expression. Mouths agape, no trace of eyelids, eyebrows raised so high they faded into the hairlines. We'd been smacked with a fistful of shock.

"I know," Abel's mother said. "I know. It's horrible. I just wanted to give Abel a nice, neat answer he'd understand. I wanted him to think his father had a good reason for never coming to visit. But Abel was almost grown up. When he got old enough, he decided to visit the man himself. So that's what he did. He came here to rescue his father."

Abel's mother stopped and looked around then, maybe searching for a sign of sympathy. No luck. Her crowd was made up of Israelis and Israelis, all our bullshit aside, don't lie. That's an American trait.

"I don't know how well you knew him," Abel's mother continued, "but Abel wasn't what you might call the brightest bulb."

Understatement of the century, I thought, though I admit feeling bad afterward.

"So it's my fault, you see," she said, beginning to mutter her words as tears escaped her Abel-ish eyes. "I shouldn't have lied to him. I should've known he'd take everything I said so seriously."

Now the woman began to sob. It was a sad, if somewhat irritating, sight. I was antsy to hear the rest of the story.

"When Abel found out about his father," she said after calming down a bit, "he went to meet him. And..."

Then she left the podium and sat down.

I could put the rest of the pieces together. Abel obviously hadn't gotten the warmest of welcomes from his would-be-war-hero father. It must have been quite upsetting. And it couldn't have made matters better being thrown into jail a few hours later for being caught AWOL. The last straw, I suspect, took place when he returned to the army only to be denied his leave. The poor idiot must have believed that when they told him, "No," he couldn't go home for his vacation; that they meant he couldn't go home ever. The army has a way of misleading people that way—making them feel hopeless. It's just that Abel took it to heart.

For the very first time, I sort of felt sorry for the guy. And I felt sorry for every one of these lone soldiers, these duped idealists who'd been conditioned to think that joining a foreign army would be meaningful and important. I felt sorry for how used they'd been by this heartless army and its number-hungry bureaucrats and how empty they'd been left. And I believed, with all my heart, that to be a lone soldier meant to be the bravest, most stupid person alive and that Abel must have been the most brave and stupid of them all.

I walked up to his grave after the service. I took a look at his weeping mother, at the confused Israeli soldiers, and then at the dead American's grave, and feeling sorrier for Abel than I did for his mother, I let out a low whistle and thought up my own eulogy:

Rest in peace Abel. You poor son of a bitch.

OPERATION GET SOME: PART I

It was not the first time Yoav had used his gun to get some.

He had been at it for a while, in fact—the semi-ingenious, semi-despicable scheme for getting into the pants of many a dumb American Jewess. It took three things: 1. the famous olive green uniform. 2. an impressive know-how for Jerusalem's tourist traps and most important: 3. the beloved M-16, fully accessorized with a series of useless jet-black gadgets. He called the gun "Luck" and always referred to it as her. So we will too.

Now, on this particular afternoon Luck was as ever at Yoav's side. She complimented him well, really; the protruding charging handle having spent so much time resting and pressing upon a slight beneath his hip that two and a half years into his service there lay an indentation on the spot. The two were like lovers conceding to one another's own permanents. He held her absent-mindedly, his palm pressed to the handle's worn-off grip as his orange hungry eyes darted about in carnal pursuit. He waited. He watched them pour out of the *shuk*, the clogged pickpocket heaven of a market without any idea of where they were heading: right towards him.

His phone rang.

"Aaron," Yoav answered in English, "You in Jerusalem?"

"Yes," the caller, this Aaron said, "but that's not what I'm calling abo—"

"Good, come down to the shuk. It's amazing. I think the pussy outnumbers the produce."

"I can't, man."

"Sure you can. Meet me on Bezalel in a half an hour."

"Yoav, listen!"

Yoav stopped. Aaron paused a second, sighed then spoke.

"Never mind."

"Good," Yoav said. "So you'll be my wingman?"

"I think you're getting better at this shit than me."

Yoav couldn't help himself from smiling.

"Learned from the best, Mr. Klotsky," he said.

"See you soon."

Aaron hung up first. For a moment Yoav stared at the phone in his hand, the other fidgeting with Luck's handle reflexively. He considered the strange distress he had detected in the words and hesitations of his friend, then disregarded it. If there was anybody he could depend on it was Aaron Klotsky, the mastermind himself of the games Yoav had been playing so long now.

It was a combination of the guy's insatiable libido and his ability to channel that drive into smooth, sweet-talking cunning that had made him a legend in the eyes of all his Israeli disciples. In particular was Yoav, a full-blown convert from the cute just-friends type to sex-slathered god. He owed it all to his scarily smart friend, as blonde as half the broads he bagged. Yoav would often say that for a lone soldier, for that's what they called them, Aaron always seemed the least lonely guy in the world.

Sure, it took a while to grow accustomed to Aaron's indifference to the other gender's feelings. Yoav had initially found the whole practice too foul and unethical to stomach despite its perks. But then the perks became the whole point. Because there is a truth about the army you must understand.

Living for twenty-one days at time on a god-forsaken base without a single female in sight does something to a man. It makes him hunger. It makes him desperate for the tender, and thus consider extremes he would never contemplate otherwise. In a word, it makes him animal. This truth was what changed Yoav. And while a part of him hated himself for participating in these calculated bouts of chauvinism, a larger part needed them.

Which brings us back to that fateful day, the one that began at the vantage point outside the shuk. There Yoav stood in uniform, majestic as a Michelangelean, returning the cell phone to his left pant pocket and refocusing his jack-o-lantern eyes on what really mattered: the tourists.

Now if poor Luck knew she was being used for something other than shooting targets and the intimidation of would-be-terrorists, she didn't show it. As far as Yoav was concerned, the gun was whatever he wanted her to be and in this case that was a magnet.

Tourists, especially the young gullible female type, were powerless to resist Luck. The gun was like a pulsing artificial light beckoning them, these flies only half-aware it meant their doom. They were drawn to the appearance of an ideal man, a soldier of the little country they'd been told to love their entire lives. Yoav was Israeli; he was a warrior and he was more a man than any of the college boys back home could ever hope to be. But most importantly, he was dangerous.

So they were drawn. First there were the two blonde sisters (Christians, he figured). One giggled. The other did the talking.

"Could we take a picture with you?"

You could do a lot more than that with me, Yoav thought.

"Sure," is what he said.

After obliging them, he moved on. There was an inquisitive family who marveled at his expertise with English. He ditched them quick despite enjoying this nourishment to his ego. Then an Israeli he mistook for a tourist. And then an early jackpot: a Birthright group. It took all the physical power Yoav could muster not to melt on the spot as these dozen American college girls—virgins to the Promised Land—violated him with their eyes.

But this Birthright group, like all the others before it, had Birthright guards, soldiers just like himself, many a man-hating fembot amongst them, who were well aware of Yoav's games. These girl soldiers could be difficult to spot—dressing like citizens, seamlessly infiltrating the ranks of hot tourists, keeping a sharp eye out for vultures like Yoav.

He'd either have to be crafty or let them pass. So he chose the latter, feeling an unusual reluctance to settle for any easy girl. Normally he would have bagged that kind in a heartbeat but not today. Something was different.

And then all of a sudden the mysterious source of his hesitation became known. He'd been waiting for someone like her.

It was the neck he noticed first. Her face turned to the side, spine rotating to accommodate whatever it was that held her interest; he couldn't name the muscle that shot out from her neck like a lonely mountain ridge, violent and elegant simultaneously. But it caught him, it the first physical suggestion of her grace, later the most vividly remembered detail she'd shed. Then its distinction recessed as her neck straightened, revealing at last her face.

One could waste a million adjectives and half a lifetime attempting to describe this sort of beauty. So I won't and Yoav certainly wasn't going to try. He just marveled at the impassioned green in her eyes and the full lips and the way her long auburn hair swayed in tune with her motion, her curiously unhurried stride. She was not just a girl. She was a woman, a beautiful one that seemed by her very posture complete. This is why Yoav should have left her alone.

But he did not do so. Instead, the makings of a plan began to form in the mind of Yoav. He considered the various methods, their possible outcomes and eventually concluded that he would have to act fast and use the oldest trick in the book. Take a chance he normally wouldn't. So Step One of Operation Get Some commenced.

Yoav walked to a fruit vendor and bought a bag of apples for three shekels. Then he went on to buy a few pitas at another stand. He cared less about the contents than he did about the bags. They meant he was, like all the other normal people, at the shuk to buy food. And of course the bags were the key to Step Two: the meeting.

He walked and bumped his way through the hordes of tourists until he was only a few meters away from the girl. Here came the tricky part. To fake clumsiness, let alone a planned collision, is no easy feat. But it was now or never, no time to play it gingerly. He made a little to the left of her in an apparent rush and just as their shoulders touched, he knocked his bags against her exposed leg, releasing them, sending the irrelevant contents flying. To say the least, it worked. Hook, line and sinker.

"Oh—*slicha!*" she exclaimed, light on the throat clearing "ch".

Definitely American, he thought. *And how charming of her to try his native tongue!*

"It's okay," he said, bending down to pick up his bags. "It's just some fruit and bread."

She lowered herself too and helped him collect the scattered food.

She began, "Ani—"

"You can speak English," he said, throwing her a playful grin. "It helps me learn."

"Sounds like you don't need much teaching," she replied, reaching for a pita and attempting to brush the dirt off it. She hadn't looked him in the eye yet.

"What I was going to say," she said, "was sorry for running into you.'"

"Not your fault—mine," he said, admitting, in a way, the truth. "I can be a real klutz."

Now she looked at him and what he saw there, beset beneath the color of her moss green eyes, was a brimming intelligence. It was foreign to him and intimidating as hell. But Yoav liked a challenge. Steady eye contact; seemed she was searching for something in his own orange pair. He did his best attempt at sincerity.

"Thanks for your help."

She considered Yoav for a moment more and there was a shift in her expression that he could not decipher. Before he could dwell any longer on its meaning, she stood up and handed over the few pitas to him. He rose and accepted them with one hand, the other subconsciously throwing Luck behind his back as if to hide her envy of the real girl.

"You're welcome," she said, "but you should probably buy some new ones."

This was the turning point and Yoav knew it. Stage Three was crossing that fine boundary between a passing acquaintance and a continued interest. It was the riskiest step yet, and the most important. Just as she seemed about ready to continue on her merry way, he acted.

"That vendor there," he nodded, pointing a finger across his chest to their left, "That's the one you want."

She cocked her head a bit confused.

"Sorry?" she said.

"That guy screaming out 'fresh bananas!' over there; he sells the best lettuce."

She frowned.

"How did you know I was looking for lettuce?"

"You really want to know?" he began with a cheeky smirk. Then he shrugged. "Just a good guess."

He let the cocky aura deflate rather suddenly, self-abasement being his best means of endearing himself to her. She had to think that his cockiness was just a cover; that he was as self-deprecating as all the other good guys out there supposedly were.

He explained: "Most Americans carrying around a bottle of vinaigrette plan to make a normal, decent salad with leaves. But they don't sell much lettuce here."

This was the moment of truth. Would she play along or would she walk away? Her hesitation and the knowing gaze she wore had him sure that this time it'd be the latter. But then to his great surprise and carnal delight, her eyes eased, the corners of her mouth bent, and she was smiling a laughing smile.

"You think you're pretty smart, huh?" she asked.

And like that Yoav knew he had her.

RIGHTEOUS MAN

"In a desert land he found him, in a barren and howling waste." –Deuteronomy, 32:10

A sweaty pair of *payot* decorate the sides of the bald, sun-burned skull. A thin-lipped mouth shaped in permanent disapproval crunches some peanuts into mush and salt. Knuckles sagging in crocodile skin tug on the fringes of the white ritualistic garment.

Yehuda has had better days.

He slouches there on his little wooden stool with an ancient siddur in his lap. He sways back and forth, mumbling the holy words by heart, eyes paying no attention to the text itself. Prayer is the last thing on Yehuda's mind. His attention is more occupied by the three talkative guests who sit across from him.

How dare they, his inner voice hisses. *Who do they think they are, barging into my home, the home I built with my own two hands, letting me serve them coffee, only to tell me this!*

Yehuda snatches the peanuts and hurls them into his mouth. Gnashing them with his tombstone teeth, he eyes the soldiers.

The handsome one, Yehuda deduces, must be the mefaked. The three blue stripes on each sleeve and his overall air of self-importance give it away. Next to him is a boyish looking soldier, big-eyed and covered in peach fuzz, whom Yehuda writes off as the weakling. As for the third, he wears on his skull a kippah and on his cheeks a trimmed beard. Religious it seems. Yehuda dislikes this one immediately—resenting his Zionistic sympathies and negligible sideburns. Nothing like a wishy-washy Jew to ruin one's morning.

The mefaked notices Yehuda watching them.

"Yehuda?" he asks. "Have you finished praying? Can we speak with you now?"

Yehuda grunts to indicate his agreement.

"Great," the mefaked says. "We have a very important issue to talk to you about."

You knew this would happen, Yehuda, he tells himself. *You knew that one day these soldiers visiting you on their patrols would barge in and rip you away from here. You knew that one day they'd come here to destroy your home.*

"We are here," the mefaked continues, "to inform you that we can no longer bring you food and water."

"Or the occasional pastry," the weakling chimes in.

"Right," says the mefaked. "Or pastries."

"What?!" Yehuda exclaims, taken aback.

"We know that you and your young friend, Avram, are quite dependent upon the army's generosity, but due to—"

"The army's generosity?!" Yehuda cries out. "Dependent?!"

"Right," the mefaked nods. "That's what I'm—"

"Who do you think you are, preaching to me about dependence?! This plot of land was barren desert before I showed up! I built this house with my bare hands, all by my very self, with nobody's help but mine!"

"Didn't Avram help?" asks the weakling, boldly.

Yehuda snorts.

"Where is Avram anyway?" the heretic asks.

"Outside," says Yehuda. "Working."

The weakling whistles between his teeth. "In this heat?" he asks. "Poor guy."

The mefaked tsks at the weakling, then turns back to Yehuda.

"Listen," he starts. "The reason we can't bring you supplies anymore is—"

"What do I care?" Yehuda barges in. "I never asked for your precious hand-me-downs, your charity. I've never needed your help."

"But you didn't mind taking it either, did you?" the weakling asks, smirking.

Yehuda cannot contain himself any longer. "Out!" he screams, leaping up and pointing to the door. "Get out of my house!"

The two soldiers glance at their mefaked. He shrugs, and nods his head toward the exit. They get up and shuffle away, ducking their heads down to avoid the low roof. The mefaked follows suit. Just as he reaches the edge of the house, he turns to Yehuda once more.

"I'd like to apologize if I offended you," he says.

Yehuda's response is to snort and stiffen his upper lip.

"You should know," the mefaked continues, "that from now on, we are forbidden to bring supplies to you or anybody in the Shilo area. It's the new rule for every unit stationed in the West Bank."

Curiosity wins over his crossness.

"Why is that?" Yehuda mutters.

"Our government is concerned with how the deliveries will be interpreted. They don't want people thinking that the army supports the…eh, legitimacy of the illegal outposts."

Yehuda grunts to indicate his indignation.

"Be grateful, Yehuda," the mefaked says. "We may return here one day with worse news."

The mefaked says this almost wistfully. His eyes wander around the walls as if they were those of doomed Jericho.

"You are disgraces," Yehuda says under his breath. "Disgraces."

The mefaked glances with pity at the old sun-burned man; Yehuda glowers in response, despising this condescension. He spits on the floor. The mefaked nods.

"Right," he says. "Goodbye then."

The mefaked walks through the doorway, leaving Yehuda alone with his holy books and bottom-burned coffee. He hears Avram outside speaking with the soldiers as they enter their Hummer. He hears alarm in the boy's voice and then panic. Avram pleads with the soldiers. They just say: "Sorry, Avram. Nothing we can do."

The car's doors slam shut, the engine starts with a roar and then Avram bursts into the house, madder than Pinhas.

"You!" he screams, pointing his dirty finger at Yehuda. "You did this, didn't you?!"

Avram is fifteen years old, if Yehuda reckons right. His eyes are a weak watery blue, his lips the naïve pouting sort, traits that only further emphasize Avram's adolescence. Avram's idiocy. But, Yehuda reminds himself, the boy serves his purpose. *Dimwits do make the best mules.*

"Shush, Avram," Yehuda says, swatting the air. "Go do something productive."

"What have you done, Yehuda?!" Avram cries. "We're ruined!"

Yehuda appraises the boy, weak eyes and all.

"You worry too much, Avram. I expected worse, anyway."

"Worse?! How could it possibly get any worse?!"

"How? I'll tell you how! They could have torn down our home!"

"But they're our friends. Why would—"

"Avram," Yehuda stops him, shaking his head. "Those men are not your friends. They are just pawns. They serve a regime that has no right to exist, a heretic government calling itself Jewish."

"I know, I know," Avram says, rolling his eyes. "They're just as bad as the Arabs."

"Worse even! Because Arabs don't parade around, pretending to be Jews, do they?"

"You don't need to lecture me, Yehuda! I know all this stuff."

"Then why act so betrayed?"

Avram sighs and looks down at his feet.

"They came here so often to check on us…I liked the company."

Yehuda considers the boy. He pushes his arm against the wooden stool to rise. He straightens his crooked back, brushes some peanut crumbs off his blue khaki pants and then lays a hand on Avram's shoulder.

"My young friend," Yehuda says. "The only company you need is that of God."

Outside they call them settlements. They say it with a sneer or a grimace, like settlements are something to be ashamed of. Yehuda stares out at them, these gated communities scattered across the desert, bordering Arab villages like the front lines of an army, and he shakes his head. *That's what the world doesn't understand*, Yehuda tells himself. *Judea is ours and we are the guardians.*

A gust of wind and sand flurries into Yehuda's face, making him cough and spit. He turns around, wipes his face, looks back at his own settlement-to-be and relishes the sight. So far, a single-room house, a leaning water tower, a stable occupied by Rushka the goat, and a rubble road make up what will one day be B'nei Eli.

So what if he didn't buy the land? So what if they call him "squatter"? As he watches Avram lug plywood, rearrange bricks and beg for water, Yehuda swells with pride. The two of them together are constructing the most important building of them all: a *beit-knesset*, a synagogue.

When this holy endeavor is finished, Yehuda surmises, the residency demands for B'nei Eli will skyrocket. He grunts to indicate his satisfaction. Then he walks back to his hut to proceed with the day's Torah study.

It is dusk when Avram crawls into the house, looking spent, smelling of sweat and burnt skin.

"Good evening Avram," Yehuda says. "How was your day?"

Avram does not acknowledge his old companion. He just collapses onto his mattress and proceeds to unlace his boots, a worn red pair he received the fall before from some amiable (albeit deluded) soldiers. Avram pulls the left boot off and tosses it against the wall. Then the other. The whole house shakes from the impact.

He's still upset, Yehuda gathers.

"Avram," Yehuda begins gingerly, "listen to me. I know that you are angry, but—"

"You don't know anything about me," Avram says.

Such savagery! Yehuda's nostrils flare, his fists clench but his mouth remains shut. *Calm down, old man*, he tells himself. *The boy is insolent, yes, but you need him.*

"Avram," Yehuda tries again, "do you remember the day we met?"

Avram does not answer. He continues to undress.

"Your parents, they were so proud to contribute to this sacred cause."

"They're dumb Americans," Avram bursts out. "They don't know any better."

"That's no way to speak of your elders!" Yehuda cries. "Show some respect!"

Again Avram responds with silence. He grabs the bowl of water and splashes his face and under his armpits. Yehuda hesitates a moment,

45

watching him. He does not like this new tone in Avram's voice—this low callous inflection—nor the wisdom the boy's words suppose. Yehuda coughs.

"Your parents," he says. "They agreed to let you come live with me, work with me so that we might rebuild what was once ours."

Eyes suddenly alight, Yehuda grabs a Humash off the bookshelf and flips through its pages.

"Here!" he says, pointing out a certain line. "Look, Avram. Read it!"

"Not now, Yehuda," Avram says. "I'm tired."

"Avram, you must read it!"

Avram grabs a towel and dries his face and body. He does not respond. Yehuda pushes on.

"A day must be spent working and studying, Avram. Study now!"

Avram finally looks at Yehuda, then down at the Humash in his outstretched hand.

"Fine," he says. "From where are we reading?"

"Yehoshua," Yehuda responds. He points to the line. "Here."

Avram leans over and reads: "'Then...then the whole congregation of the people of Israel assembled at Shilo and set up the tent of meeting there.'"

He finishes and looks at Yehuda, his face blank.

"So?" Avram asks.

"So?!" Yehuda replies incredulously. "So, that is the whole reason we are here! The Holy of Holies itself sat here in Shilo for 369 years. This was the holy capital before Jerusalem!"

Avram nods and then continues with his routine. He grabs a torn up T-shirt and pulls it over his head. Yehuda bites his lip.

"Does this not impress you?"

Avram turns to Yehuda, his expression cold.

"How do you know this is the spot?" he asks.

Yehuda frowns. "What do you mean?"

"I mean," Avram says slowly, "how do you know this is Shilo?"

Yehuda's mouth suddenly feels dry, his tongue too large. He trips on his own words.

"This...this is Shilo," Yehuda stutters. "It has been studied and agreed upon."

"Okay," Avram says. "Who says?"

Yehuda stares at the boy as if for the first time. He stalls not for lack of knowledge; each geographical facet of his faith the old man committed to memory long ago. No, Yehuda refuses to answer Avram due to a long dormant fear. The fear—no, the terror that the pupil might discern the symptoms of his teacher's ancient sickness, his doubt.

The question, "Who says?" is one of many to which the scholarly replies always rang, to Yehuda's ears, as deceptive validations. Ruses to keep clever inquiries quiet. He cannot possibly recite these answers now without revealing his incertitude. For a moment, the briefest moment, Avram seems to see the discord stirring within Yehuda's eyes. Yehuda sees Avram, sees as the boy reads his old master, and thinks to himself, *I underestimated him*. Yehuda nearly shudders at the implications.

"No more questions," Yehuda says with a start, snapping the Humash closed. "We must pray and eat supper before it is dark."

Avram's eyelids contract into a suspicious glare. Yehuda dares not address the boy's defiance. He will not allow that old fear to rear its head again. He breaks eye contact, places the holy book upon the bench and rises.

"Come now, Avram," Yehuda says, facing the bookshelf. "You shall be the first to guard tonight."

Yehuda hears Avram hesitate for a second too long, then turn and shuffle off into his corner. Yehuda lies down upon his mattress and, with the corner of his eye, he watches his young disciple, who hitherto he believed so submissive.

Yehuda grunts once again to indicate his chagrin but assures himself. *Even mules must think.*

Sunlight tickles the eyelids of the old man. They twitch, twitch again and then the eyes blink slowly open, perceiving rays of light athwart the ceiling. *This is odd*, Yehuda thinks. *It should still be dark.* He turns his head toward Avram's mattress. Empty.

Yehuda gets up slowly and ambles toward the door. He opens it and squints his eyes as the dazzling summer dawn greets him.

"Avram!" he yells out. "Avram, why didn't you wake me?"

He probably fell asleep with the goat again, Yehuda surmises. Shielding his eyes with his hairy forearm, Yehuda approaches the stable.

"Avram!" he yells out. "Wake up!"

As Yehuda enters the stable, the goat bleats and stamps its hooves.

"Shush, Rushka," he says. "Shush. Where is your favorite?"

Yehuda walks out. He does a lap around the small settlement. He checks the water tower, the road and the house again but finds no sign of Avram.

"Avram!" he yells out. He walks to the edge of the mountain and shouts again.

"Avram!"

The desert wind swallows his voice. He stands there motionless, staring out at the desert beneath him, at the villages Duma and Jalud, at the green minarets of their mosques. His eyes follow the mud-caked Hummers, busy circling around their army garrisons like a group of starved buzzards. Then he sees the settlements Shilo and Adei Ad in the distance, sees their tall security fences and the long dusty roads in between them. He nods his head. Shvut Rachel.

Two kilometers away upon a yellow hill covered in shrubs and untamed olive trees, in between Shilo and Adei Ad, sits the small settlement known by this name. Yehuda journeys there on occasion to pick up supplies and to scowl at the "orthodox-lite" occupants. They are as fond of Yehuda as he is of them. But some young men do approach Avram, converse with the boy, smile and ask him to join their football matches.

Avram fancies their attention too much for Yehuda's comfort. These people and their pick-and-choose practice of Judaism might seduce the impressionable boy. So on their last visit, just a week before, Yehuda forbade the boy from ever going to Shvut Rachel again. He claimed that Rushka needed his company. Ever since then, Avram seethed, occasionally erupting into mutinous tirades, not unlike those from the preceding evening.

Now, staring out at the settlement in the distance, Yehuda understands. He need not play detective any longer. He must delay B'nei Eli's construction, travel to Shvut Rachel and liberate Avram of those depraved people's influence. Of this, Yehuda is certain.

"Rushka," Avram says under his breath, walking toward the stable. "We have a holy errand ahead of us."

They stare. All of them stare at the dusty old man and the goat tethered to his hand. He can practically hear their tongues curling words into defamations; smell the stench upon their recreant breath. Could Yehuda curse these so-called Jews, he would.

He walks along the sidewalk, past houses with red-brick roofs and grassy front yards and children playing duck-duck-goose. He passes two indecently dressed women with strollers who chatter in English. *Typical*, he thinks.

Yehuda reaches the small convenience store, attaches Rushka to a pole outside and enters.

"Baruch?" he says, looking behind the empty counter. "Is anybody here?"

A door to the storage closet opens and a heavyset man with a neatly trimmed beard shuffles in. He forces a smile at the sight of this visitor.

"Yehuda," says Baruch. "Back so soon?"

At least he attempts to be civil, Yehuda considers, though the hushed discomfort in the fat man's voice is unmistakable.

"Hello Baruch," Yehuda answers, tone detached. "I'm looking for my boy, Avram."

"Avram?"

"Yes," Yehuda says impatiently. "Avram."

"I saw him here with you about two weeks ago," says Baruch. "But since then?"

Baruch shakes his head and, involuntarily, his waddle. Grunting, Yehuda glances around the small convenience store.

"You should try the basketball court," says Baruch. "Some of his friends may be there."

"His friends?"

Baruch opens his mouth to respond, then closes it.

"Where is this court?" asks Yehuda.

The young men dash back and forth along the asphalt, their kippahs fastened onto their skulls by stalwart bobby pins. The odd man standing at the sidelines attempts to clear his throat for a second time.

"Ahem!" says Yehuda. "Where is Avram?"

One boy whose jaw juts violently far beyond his face fixes his gaze upon Yehuda for a moment. The ball sits in his hands. Somebody yells at him to pass it so he turns back. He passes the ball to a ginger, who sprints toward the hoop.

"Avram," Yehuda repeats. "He is here, is he not?"

The ginger shoots the ball and misses. It bounces off the rim into a sea of violent arms and somebody's hand slaps it out of bounds. The ginger runs off to collect the ball. As the rest of the kids settle, Yehuda strides onto the court with Rushka in tow. He approaches the boy with the under-bite.

"You," Yehuda says, pointing his finger. "Tell me. Where is he?"

"Who?" the under-bite asks, panting.

"Avram."

"Get that goat off the court."

"Where is Avram?" Yehuda asks more forcefully.

"Who's Avram?" the under-bite asks.

"My boy," says Yehuda. "You spoke with him two weeks ago. I saw you two."

The kid shoots a scrutinizing look at Yehuda and then nods his head slowly.

"Yeah," he says. "Okay. I think I remember him. He works for you, right?"

"He is here?"

Just then the ginger returns with the ball and the under-bite shrugs.

"Good luck finding him," he says, turning back toward his friends.

The ginger hurls the basketball to another boy and they all begin to race around the court again. Soon the ball greets the hands of the under-bite, who turns to pivot and stops abruptly. The goat stands there impassive before his legs.

"Sir?" he says, glancing down at Rushka, then up at Yehuda. "Are you planning on moving?"

"You have seen Avram," Yehuda says. "One of you. I am sure of it."

The under-bite rolls his eyes and looks at the others. Somebody laughs.

"Avram isn't here," the kid says slowly, pronouncing his words. "Now will you please move?"

Yehuda does not dignify this with a response.

"You need to go now," the under-bite says through his misplaced clenched teeth.

He rests the basketball against his hip with his elbow. Yehuda stands his ground, glaring at all the kids of different ages and observances. Some more religious. Some less. This one with the flapping jaw, decidedly less.

"What's wrong with you?" asks the under-bite with perturbed curiosity.

"With me?" Yehuda asks, horrified. "Is it I who has forsaken *halacha* as a passing whim, who has betrayed our commandments for modern idols? Is it I who purports decency and then eyes with avarice the world's sinners; embraces each strange Lilith as one would a mother? Dare, tell me, do I pride myself a Jew and then endorse this Zionist nightmare, culpable every day it exists for the Moshiach's absence?!"

The under-bite gapes at the old man, who almost froths from the mouth in his severity.

"What is wrong with me," Yehuda says, his voice quieter, but his eyes still alight, "is that I fear God."

Then he sneers and waves his finger toward the under-bite and his friends.

"You, all of you self-proclaimed pious, you may be Jews by blood. But you're no better than the goyim. Counterfeits."

Yehuda spits this last word into the under-bite's face. The under-bite hesitates a moment, forcing himself to forestall his outrage. He wipes the saliva off his cheek, glances back at his friends, shrugs, and then bursts out into foreboding laughter. He chucks the ball to the ginger, leans down toward the goat, grabs the animal's collar and jerks her by the neck.

"What are you doing?!" Yehuda cries.

"Getting your damn goat off our court," the under-bite replies, pulling the goat and Yehuda along with her toward the grass.

"Get your hands off of her!" Yehuda yells, yanking the leash.

The goat bleats frantically and bucks her head as the men pull her neck back and forth. Laughing, the boy looks toward his friends.

"Will somebody help me with this guy already?"

Two kids walk over; one pulls Yehuda off the court by his shoulder. The other, the ginger, pries his hand off the leash.

"Disgraces!" he shrieks. "You call yourself Jews?! Disgraces!"

The boys all laugh. They get the old man and his goat off the court and shove him toward the road.

"Your boy's not here," the under-bite says. "Go away before we call security."

Yehuda's eyes are those of a feral animal's, his forehead's bulging veins the mangrove's roots. He grabs Rushka's leash.

"You are all sick!" he shrieks.

The boys pick up the basketball and resume their game. Yehuda remains staring, enraged and yet perplexed. *Where is that boy?* he asks himself.

Yehuda watches the young settlers of Shvut Rachel a moment longer, then turns around and walks toward the road. Glancing at all these cookie-cutter houses, Yehuda sighs. *So many doorbells to ring*, he thinks.

Just then, the door of Baruch's store opens. The same two women with the strollers saunter out, prattling again in their native tongue. English. Some tickling sensation overcomes Yehuda. Avram's parents. The Americans from Halamish.

Yehuda smiles serenely, glances down at Rushka and pats her head. "One more detour," he tells the goat.

There is a highway numbered 443 upon which only Israelis drive. The Palestinian and the anti-Zionist Jew (Yehuda included) call it the apartheid road. This is where the buses run from settlement to settlement, where the military's armored cars constantly patrol, and where Yehuda finds himself hiking with his goat a day after their excursion in Shvut Rachel.

Yehuda walks along the edge of the best-paved road in the West Bank and he stares at the stubby mountain before him. Halamish, that behemoth of a settlement, poses a very acute climb. They might not make it by dusk. *Avram*, he asks himself, *why did you abandon me now?*

He met the boy over a year ago in Nahliel, one of the few settlements built and maintained by—in Yehuda's eyes—like-minded men. Righteous men. Yehuda had visited this place on occasion to meet with the Rebbe Kahan and, when the time had come to realize B'nei Eli, to find an apprentice. Kahan recommended a sagacious boy in his Yeshiva, a learned youth with dark excitable eyes and small teeth by the name of Zohar.

Zohar, Yehuda recognized in the first few minutes of their interview, was a true anomaly. He possessed a fearsome, nearly defiant acumen and harbored the ambition to not merely speak, but to deliver words with the same gravitas of the Choze Lublin.

The thirteen-year-old boy shook Yehuda to his core. After Zohar, he knew both what genius in the flesh resembled, and what nature he did not desire in a prospective apprentice.

No, he wanted Zohar's schoolmate, the boy with the god-fearing eyes and dumb pouting lips, the one they called Avram. Understanding Yehuda's intentions, Rebbe Kahan spoke.

"Friend," Kahan told Yehuda, "do not mistake the appearance for the essence of a man."

He warned Yehuda that Avram was sharper than he appeared, that the physical attribute did not always reflect what lay within.

"You will be disappointed," Kahan said.

But this advice, Yehuda dismissed.

He met Avram's parents in Halamish. He sat for an hour and a half in their home, suffering their mispronunciations of the language and misinterpretations of the mitzvot. The mother was reluctant but the father, whose eyes Avram had obviously inherited, was dense and easily swayed. After many assurances and pious lectures, Yehuda received their permission. Avram was to join him in the barren hills of Shilo. They were to build B'eni Eli together.

He believed that the boy would always obey him.

"How…disappointing," Yehuda mutters to himself. Then he spits into the sand.

The night approaches fast. What remains of the day are the edges of the sun upon the jagged cliffs above, yet Yehuda and his goat stand far below. He knows where he must advance but he hesitates.

There are caves, they say, where young religious men conspire in the dark. Not enough men for a minyan; they disown this ritual for a holier endeavor, just as Moshe Rabbeinu forsook his flock. The *sikrikim*. They will host Yehuda, if he can find them. If it is his wish to find them.

He leaves behind the highway and follows an indistinct dirt path. He walks forward. Shrubs and tumbleweeds latch onto and slip off his blue khaki pants. The trail leads toward a black chasm in the mountain that appears all the blacker as the first stars in the sky emerge. Yehuda eases to a stop and peers into the cave. So dense is the shade within, so depthless. He tugs nervously on his grey saltbush beard and Rushka bleets.

"Shush Rushka," he whispers to the goat. "There is no need to be afraid."

But Yehuda cannot bring himself to move forward. There are other stories told about these young men, cruel aspersions cast no doubt to inspire such misgivings, but which nonetheless disquiet Yehuda.

A high-pitched howl sounds in the distance, then another. Yehuda feels his old bones shiver within his skin and tries to calm himself. He knows the source well. Golden jackals often abound in these parts. Still, Yehuda's feet tread backward, lean away from the black hole.

We shall walk, he tells himself. *Save time.*

Pulling Rushka's leash closer to him, Yehuda turns around and hustles away. He walks a hundred paces, resisting the temptation to look over his shoulder. Eyes watch him; he can feel them piercing into his bent back. He comes to a standstill, he breathes and then he turns his head to stare at the cave.

What he sees is the face of the mountain and nothing more. No strangers' eyes. No ghosts of Endor. No greedy jackal. Yehuda grunts, shakes his head and walks onward to the apartheid road.

To Halamish.

"What do you mean, 'Where is Avram?'"

Yehuda's eyes glaze over a moment. Once again he sits upon the American couple's couch. He struggles to remain conscious as Avram's parents gaze at him intently, awaiting an answer. The boy's mother is as immodest as ever. Her swollen belly suggests yet another pregnancy; a newborn lies in her arms and a two-year-old crawls along the floor. *They follow that mitzvah well*, Yehuda gathers.

"Avram," he finally responds. "He came to you."

"No," the mother says. "He is with you."

Yehuda looks down at the ground and clenches his jaw. He does not register these words because they belong to a woman. She knows better than to speak to him.

"Please," Yehuda says, addressing the man. "Remind your wife to reserve her outbursts for your consumption."

The man looks at his wife, cheeks blushed in her outrage, and touches her hand gently. He gestures toward the doorway, nodding. She pulls her hand out of his, stands up stiffly and storms out of the room, only stopping to scoop up the toddler. The father sighs, his feeble eyes misty.

"Forgive her," he says. "The children make her weary."

"Praise God, those are the extent of her crises," Yehuda responds.

The father nods solemnly.

"Where were we?" Yehuda asks.

"Avram," the father says, his strong "r" reminding Yehuda of the man's American origin.

Yehuda nods and says, "Yes, your boy. As you very well know, he deserted me. I assume he craved familial comforts. Still, you should not have indulged him."

"What?!" the father asks, his pink face draining of color.

Truly a family of fools! Yehuda loathed all repetition but prayer.

"Where is the boy?" Yehuda asks.

"You are his guardian," the father stammers. "He is supposed to be with you!"

Yehuda tsks. "No, no. He was with me. He returned here."

"He did not!" the father cries.

Yehuda rubs his eyes and looks at the father, squinting.

"How can this be?"

"You tell me!" the father says. "He lives with you!"

"No," Yehuda says, grinding his grey teeth. "He lived with me. That is, until the day he decided to run off."

"What makes you so sure?!" the father asks frantically. "How do you know he hasn't been taken?!"

Yehuda hesitates. His mouth gapes open and very slightly his right eyebrow lifts.

"I..." he says, his voice hollow, "I hadn't considered it."

Now the father's eyes, once so meek, bulge out of their sockets. He leaps out of his seat and seizes Yehuda by his suit jacket with clenched fists. "How long now?!" he screams, shaking him hard.

"Three—" Yehuda stammers. "Three days."

"You good-for-nothing!" the father cries, pulling Yehuda up to his face. "You've lost my son!"

Yehuda tries to pry the father's paws off, while the mother rushes into the room.

"What—what are you doing?!" she shrieks, running toward their tangled arms.

"He's lost our son!" the father screams. "Our Avram!"

Stunned, the wife freezes. The father loosens his grip of Yehuda's jacket, steps backward and then collapses into his seat. He covers his face in his hands, his shoulders grow taut and a low moan escapes his lips. Yehuda senses the petrified woman staring but refuses to meet her eyes. He brushes off his coat and glances at the father.

"I..." he says, trailing off, "I will find your son."

Then Yehuda turns around and bolts out of the house before either can say another word.

Could it be? He asks himself. *Could Avram really have been kidnapped?*

He unties Rushka and glances behind furtively at the house. The door is shut, but behind the bay window, pulling back the curtain with her hand, stands Avram's mother. For once Yehuda looks at her and, meeting her wide eyes for the first time, the old man shudders. Repulsion, he has known. Disinterest, dislike, disrepute; he has known them all. But never until this moment, has Yehuda known hatred.

With the goat's leash in hand, he turns and forces his tired legs to amble away. At the yellow gates of Halamish, Yehuda stops to stare out into the Judean and Samarian desert. He is Jacob, the wilderness his scheming sons. He stands, stripped of his schemes and beggared of inklings. The boy he promised to shelter is lost.

Yehuda covers his eyes with the palm of his pockmarked hand. A gnawing feeling, an ache, so foreign to Yehuda, seizes him. Uninvited and involuntary, it alters his haughty countenance into a pained grimace.

This, Yehuda gathers, *this must be guilt.*

When the flame of the campfire flickers, the old man hugs his shoulders and shivers in his sleep. When the fire dies, he awakens. The pitiless wind whips every exposed sliver of his skin; it creeps under his makeshift suit blanket and chills his iron joints. Between two large malaki stones in the mountainside of Halamish, here the trembling Yehuda rouses.

He glances at the ash and groans, readjusting the jacket on his torso. *Perhaps Rushka can shield the storm,* he thinks.

"Rushka," he calls out. "Rushka, come here."

He should know better. The goat is not a dog. He turns his head to look at her.

"Rushka?" he asks the wind.

What he sees is the bruised blue horizon and nothing more. He picks himself up slowly and gazes around.

"Rushka!" he calls out.

Now he hears in the distance a high-pitched baying. Or is it just the wind whistling? Yehuda listens a moment longer and then, certain what he hears is the goat, the old man jumps up and begins to jog toward her.

His knees throb as he pummels his feet into the rocky mountainside. The pitch of the goat's cry ascends and ascends until it no longer resembles the yelp of an animal but the shriek of a human child. Yehuda begins to run.

"I'm coming!" he yells out.

Yehuda can sense he is close. He stops to scan the mountainside below him and then he spots it. Not it, no. Them. Below, maybe two hundred meters away, three slinky black shapes dance around a collapsed figure, whose contours, though shrouded in the dark, are unmistakable to its master.

"Rushka!" Yehuda exclaims. He tears down the mountain, avoiding as best he can the jagged malaki stone. The goat screeches louder and longer than ever before, then hiccups violently. Silence follows. *Lord,* Yehuda pleads, *I need her!*

He sees them now, sees their thin limbs, the tremor in their necks. Their heads are close together, bent down and gyrating. Feeding.

"NO!" he screams.

The golden jackals' heads spin toward him, their slit-eyes glowing in the moonlit shade. Unflinching, they stare at the advancing man.

"Get off of her!" Yehuda shouts out, flailing his arms in the air.

The jackals gingerly retreat their steps, shining eyes still fixed upon Yehuda.

"I said, go!" he shouts again, now only a few meters away.

The closest jackal growls and bares his teeth and Yehuda sees the blood swimming within those jaws. He opens his mouth to shout and then swallows it as his leg catches upon an upturned rock, catapulting him forward. He floats for a moment and then plummets into the desert floor. Sand shoots into the heavens, rocks scatter.

Yehuda lies there, groaning, and vaguely discerns the sound of the jackals' feet scampering away. After some time, he lifts himself up and touches his leg. There is a cut there, attracting his body's heat, oozing a wet metallic liquid.

The blood reminds him. Yehuda squints forward in the dark and sees the shape of goat a few meters away.

"Rushka?" he asks.

She neither moves nor bleats nor, from Yehuda's vantage point, appears to breathe. He pulls himself up and limps toward her.

"Rushka," he says, "it is alright. You will be…"

Yehuda sees the goat clearly, fixes his gaze upon her torn out throat and splayed, steaming innards. He gags, turns away and kneels down. He tries to breathe, gags again and then vomits.

Yehuda looks back at the dead goat. He turns his eyes away and feels their corners sting. His eyes, so long two dry wells, begin to water. Could Yehuda curse, he would curse this irrepressible effect. Weakness is for others, not for him. But even as he thinks this, a single tear trails down his dirty left cheek.

He dares not look above. He does not ask God, "Why?" He will not beg. Instead, Yehuda, wilted by his injury, stands up slowly and limps away. He climbs down the mountain, telling his troubled mind that the goat was a sacrifice.

God demands I act alone, he thinks. *Like Jonah, I must defy the Lord's designs no longer. I must commit.*

Thus reassured, the old man ambles forward faster.

Bedouins. Russet skin, eyes of ink, long pale throbes, and worn keffiyehs. The man and women stand so still, they appear painted upon their sand-dune horizon.

Yehuda knows these people well. Their crude villages—built on foundations of rotten wood and stolen sheet metal—are strewn about every corner of the Negev. Infamous as drifters and thieves, the Bedouins are said to be the desert's eyes, observing all without ever intervening.

Yehuda never saw a reason to become acquainted with a Bedouin. No Arab ever interested him. Until now.

His entire essence is thirst. His throat is sandpaper, his lips cut, and his knuckles cracked. The wound seeps down his dull throbbing leg and dries in the hair. His feet somehow propel Yehuda forward, driven by dire need alone.

As he comes closer to their tent, he fixes his eyes upon the Bedouins. They appear to be a family. A tall male stands in the sunlight, towering overoverov the others, the females, who huddle behind in the shade upon woolen rugs.

Yehuda cannot detect if the man's rigid posture means to menace or purely self-preserve. He does not wish to test him.

"Water!" he cries out, voice wheezing. "Give me water."

Yehuda slows to a standstill twenty meters away from their tents. He attempts to gesture with his hands, gripping his throat, pointing to his mouth. The Bedouin man stares, unmoved.

"I need water," Yehuda says. "W-a-t-e-r."

The man remains still and silent. Yehuda will not ask please. He will not beg. It is beneath him, even in this state.

"You must," he says. "I am in great need."

Yehuda cannot be sure if his eyes deceive him; the weariness and thirst weigh down upon his reason, but beneath the worn red keffiyeh the Bedouin wears upon his face, Yehuda swears he sees the man spread a close-lipped smile. Amused.

"Scoundrel!" he cries. "I am your guest! Bring me water!"

He advances forward upon his left leg, forgetting his injury, and feels his knee buckle beneath him. Whatever energy Yehuda had left is spent. He falls forward into the sand and turns his cheek so that he gazes upon the dark feet of the Bedouin man. The sight is blurry, obfuscated by dust and fatigue. Faintly, he notices one foot tap the ground, as if impatient, and then step toward him.

Now the feet are two centimeters breadth from his face, fetid odor and all. Without warning, Yehuda lurches toward the tent as if being dragged. His body slides along the desert floor toward the shade of the tent. At the threshold, this same unseen source stops, grabs him by his legs and neck and hoists his body onto a cot within. His ear touches the cool metal and he shivers.

A low voice murmurs strange words marked by guttural stops and impossible fluidity.

"*Ja'la hur ha.*"

He hears other figures shuffle around. A hand touches his left leg and rips the cloth from his pant. Some leg-hairs curdled in blood rip off with it and Yehuda gasps.

He is awake. The Bedouin man sits upon a stool beside his cot, holding a shallow plastic bowl filled with water. He pours it onto the bruised gash and Yehuda swallows his breath. It is not water. It is alcohol. Judging by the licorice scent, *arak*.

He shouts, kicks his leg and thrashes around, expecting to feel arms constrain him. None do. He calms himself and opens his eyes and gazes upon the Bedouin man, who remains a calm and patient observer. A woman clad in a dark, never-ending shawl approaches the man and taps his shoulder. She holds a needle and black thread as if they were grapes served for a king.

The Bedouin snatches them out of her hands and shoos her away with a candidness Yehuda cannot help but admire. The Bedouin looks Yehuda in the eye, holds up the items in his hands, and nods his head as if to say, "May I proceed?"

Yehuda grinds his tungsten teeth and points to his mouth.

"Water?" he asks, voice rasping.

"*La'a,*" the Bedouin answers, wagging his finger side to side.

Yehuda grunts to indicate his exasperation and then, staring at the needle and thread in the Bedouin's fists, he nods his head. *Yes.*

Underneath a coverlet of city-light stars, which emerge only in these quiet hinterlands, the two men stand. The wound on Yehuda's leg, bandaged in hand-sewn cotton, bleeds through its wrappings. He gazes upon the dark, muscular stranger beside him and, despite his Muslim sacrilege, Yehuda admires the Bedouin.

Like Yehuda, the Bedouin is a man of austere values. The modesty of his wives, the command he holds over them, and his rigorous treatment of Yehuda, are each a testament to the man's profound commitment to God.

He would make a good Jew, Yehuda thinks. Then he opens his mouth to speak.

"I am looking for a boy," he says slowly.

The Bedouin meets his eyes but his face betrays no expression.

"He is lost out here," Yehuda tells the Bedouin, "somewhere in the desert alone."

Yehuda turns to stare into the wilderness.

"He could be anywhere."

He feels a hand touch his shoulder. It is the Bedouin's, who shakes his head decisively.

"Where then?" Yehuda asks, surprised.

The Bedouin remains still. His eyes shut, his forehead frowns and a hum escapes his thin lips. He sways as if entangled in some sinister trance. Yehuda cannot fathom such idolatrous rituals but the gravity of the Bedouin's prayer nevertheless impresses him. The Bedouin comes to a calm; he opens his eyes and stretches his hand out toward the east, rigid finger aligned with distant green and yellow lights. Yehuda recognizes their source.

"Duma?" Yehuda asks, aghast.

The Bedouin nods.

"How could you possibly know that?"

"*Allah ya'kul ul ya*" the Bedouin replies.

Yehuda cannot comprehend the stranger's language, religion or his assumed clairvoyance, but some primordial instinct within him urges Yehuda to trust him. He gazes out at Duma and groans. He always eyed the Palestinian village from above, from B'nei Eli's precipice. He never entertained the notion that he would one day step foot upon the land. Now that day has come.

He turns to the Bedouin and some strange compulsion overcomes him.

"Thank you," Yehuda murmurs, shocking himself.

"*B'nei Ja'a,*" the Bedouin replies.

Then he turns around and walks away. Yehuda watches the Bedouin go, watches his white throbe disappear into the distance like a reconciled spirit and the old man sighs. He checks the wound upon his leg, drinks one last sip of arak from the Bedouin's plastic bowl and delays no further.

No more sojourns. No more aberrations from the errand. Avram and Avram alone.

Yehuda discards the Bedouin's bowl, straightens his tattered jacket and directs his legs east toward the village they call Duma.

Before the ascent to Mount Nebo, before the final gaze upon the Promised Land, before the anonymous burial, Moshe Rabbeinu delivered one final lesson to the people of Israel, a condemnation and challenge that comes to Yehuda's mind as he stares into the odd amalgam of Arab faces in the dank basement of a certain house in Duma.

"'I will hide my face from them,' the LORD said…

'I will make them envious by those who are not a people;

I will make them angry by a nation that has no understanding.'"

Yehuda looks into the eyes of his suspicious hosts and recognizes within them the forewarning from the Torah. These miserable people who invent a nationality and call it Palestine, who speciously derive their namesake from the Philistines of lore, who lay claim to the land through larceny and slaughter, they are "those who are not a people," the everlasting thorn in the Israelites' side, a reminder from the Lord to never betray his mitzvot again.

And these are the same people with whom Yehuda now breaks bread. They lay a plain *musakhan* dish before him. He remembers the mitzvah of *pikuach nefesh*, and considers his starved state. The bread is unkosher. But he will surely die unless he eats. He shuts his eyes, mumbles the prayer quickly, rubs his hands together, and then proceeds to rip off an edge of the *taboon* bread without further debate.

Across from him huddle his accommodating hosts, the so-called Nusseibeh Elders. They are five pale ancient men in chess-piece color keffiyehs and all except one, glare at Yehuda as a blasphemy in need of rectification.

The tallest of the five, the exception, turns to a young cosmopolitan-looking Arab man and whispers into his ear.

"Now," translates the young man in broken Hebrew, "we have followed custom. We have fed you. We have hosted you. Talk. You must talk now. Or we will kill you where you sit, Jew."

As he recites this last sentence, the young translator's voice cracks and his posture slopes. *He is modern,* Yehuda thinks. *He is not comfortable playing this role.*

Yehuda grabs a piece of musakhan, jams it into his mouth and chews loudly. He shapes his first three fingers into a triangle and flaps his hand lazily. He expects them to understand the gesture.

"What—" the young man says. "What is this?"

Yehuda concludes his chewing and swallows. "It means," Yehuda answers, "'Wait.'"

"Perhaps I am not clear?" the young man asks.

"No, you were clear."

Yehuda takes another bite of the bread and with the corner of his eye, he watches the Elders. They glance into each other's eyes in search of meaning. *Why does the fool show no fear?* They no doubt ponder.

"Jew," the young man translates again for the tall whispering Elder. "You will die here unless you speak. Why play with your life?"

"I will speak," Yehuda grumbles through a mouthful. "But I have two demands which you must honor first."

The young man's eyes widen and he hesitates before translating. Yehuda watches closely as the five men gape in disbelief upon hearing this fresh sacrilege. One of the Elders springs to his feet and points into Yehuda's face, shrieking in Arabic. His hands are daggers and then rifles and then strung nooses, a series of harried gestures requiring no translation.

The tall Elder grabs a fistful of the man's cloak and pulls him back down to his seat. He speaks calmly into the hothead's ear and mollifies him. Despite himself, Yehuda esteems this tall Elder and the quiet wisdom with which he commands authority. The Elder then turns back to the translator.

"You do no one favors with your insolence," the young man repeats.

Hesitating, Yehuda considers the Elder carefully. Then he opens his mouth.

"My demands are as follows," he says. "One: you shall release me, unscathed, when our business is complete."

The young man whispers into the Elder's ear and then listens himself.

"You say 'release you'," the young man translates. "Do we hold you against your will?"

Clever man, Yehuda thinks. *This is not an answer.*

"Do I have your word?" he asks.

The translator need not speak. The Elder nods his head with solemn poise.

"Good," Yehuda says, nodding. "My second demand is that you free my young friend Avram."

While the boy translates, four of the Elders turn toward each other, their expressions puzzled. The fifth Elder, their tall leader gazes upon Yehuda with hushed sympathy.

"You are misled, stranger," the young surrogate says. "There is no Avram here."

Another Yehuda would have contravened this displeasing response. He would have fought these Arabs with whatever frantic logic he could muster. But the days in the desert have wearied the old man and stripped him of his wicked tongue. He opens his mouth but no sound escapes his throat.

"There is no Avram here," the translator repeats.

Yehuda looks at the tall Elder now and he reads in the man's sad eyes an inimitable truth and he believes these words with the whole of his old heart. Yehuda bows his head down and covers his face with shaking hands. *Why would the Bedouin lie?* The desperation ripples across his face. Yehuda stands not one step closer toward discovering the boy. Avram remains lost. Duma, yet another fruitless detour.

"I will go now," he whispers.

The Elder nods. Yehuda rises and looks around the dreary basement.

"Why?" he asks. "Why show me such kindness?"

The translator turns his lips to the Elder's ear and then his ear to the Elder's lips.

"This is not kindness," the young man says. "A dead Jew is not good for our village. We have enough soldiers and police coming in and out of the village since the…"

The translator's speech trails off; he turns to question the Elder in Arabic. Yehuda, meanwhile, turns his legs toward the stairs. The source of the Elder's pause concerns him not. There is only Avram, only his pursuance. Yehuda cannot bear another mystery, so he turns to depart.

He walks three paces and stops. *One last question,* he thinks.

"Tell me," Yehuda murmurs, facing the stairs. "Did a boy ever pass by here with blue eyes and red boots and small curls like these?"

He touches his grey sidecurls with the tips of his fingers and turns his head toward the Elder. He expects no recognition. It is a last desperate entreaty and nothing more. But as Yehuda looks into the Elder's eyes, his breath deserts him and his stomach drops.

The Elder's color is a dark violet hue. His veins bulge out of his forehead, his whole body trembles with suppressed rage.

"What?!" Yehuda breathes.

The Elder rises, still convulsing, and exhales long shuttering breaths. He pulls on the coat of the young translator and leans upon him for support as they approach Yehuda. Then, face to face, separated only by a finger length, Yehuda and the Elder breathe the same damp air.

"Boy," the Elder rasps himself in Hebrew. "Blue eyes."

"Yes!" Yehuda whispers, amazed. "You have…"

He goes no further. A deep murderous rage surfaces in the corners of the Elder's eyes and in the bend of his pale mouth. He points his finger to the stairs.

"Go," the translator says.

"No, please," Yehuda says and this is the first time the word escapes his mouth. "Where did you see Avram?"

The Elder speaks into the translator's ear and then fixes his eyes upon Yehuda.

"Follow me," says the young man.

The three men stare at the modern ruin. A dilapidated building, charred and leaking ash. Crooked mutilated frame. Torn paper and purple curtains covered in soot. Masses of broken alabaster marked with graffiti. Hebrew graffiti. Stars of David.

At the sight of the burnt down structure, Yehuda senses an epiphany lurking at the fringes of his mind. The story can be read within these remains. Still, he listens to the tall Elder recount the building's end.

"This is our mosque," the young man translates. "It stands here seventy years before the fire."

The noxious scent of gasoline and smoke sting Yehuda's nostrils. So fresh, this inferno.

"They come," the young man says, pausing to listen to the Elder. "The cave-dwellers. A few villagers catch sight of them as they set the building ablaze."

Yehuda turns his eyes away from the building, repulsed. The image, to him, intimates a fresh bleeding gash.

"This boy...this Avram," the translator says slowly. "The one you seek. He comes, one of these sikrikim."

Yehuda shivers.

"Those eyes," the translator follows the Elder. "The color of the Heavens."

It is Avram.

"But in their essence...the evil of djinns," the young man translates.

Yehuda stares at the mosque. The sikrikim, the same young cave-dwellers of whom Yehuda nearly dared to entreat hospitality, burnt the sanctuary to the ground. These were Avram's captors; his new shepherds. Sikrikim and Avram amongst them, the young fool. What corrupt golem

70

had Yehuda wrought upon this world? What agent of anarchy had Yehuda contrived? Yehuda stares into the cadaver of the sanctuary and feels the prickling on his nape, the same creeping on his flesh that he felt facing the cave of Halamish.

"When you come here," the Elder says through the young man, "the Elders, they plan to kill you. To avenge this devastation."

Yehuda's brain spins within his skull. He feels dizzy and ill. The tall Elder bends down upon his knees and brushes the debris away from a leather book beneath the rubble.

"It makes sense," the translator continues, "as much sense as burning down our mosque. Yet…"

The Elder pulls the leather book from the floor and examines it, brushing the dust off its cover.

"I will not allow it."

Yehuda breathes shallow as the Elder stands up to his full height and flips through pages of the discovered book.

"Look here," he says. "This is perhaps the only survivor. No, it is not holy. It is simply a ledger. Names of guests, needed provisions. Details of routine."

The Elder gently shuts the book and slides a finger down its binding.

"The book is not holy," he says, "but it is. Now it must be."

Yehuda looks at the gaunt stranger before him and is suddenly overcome by a foreign emotion. Reverence. For another man. For a people and a God contrary to his own. For the grace with which this Nusseibeh Elder endures cruelty. And for the man's compassion, at once so singular and presumed. He owes the Arab his life.

Yehuda takes a step toward the Elder.

"I am going to find Avram," he says. "I will make him repent for this evil."

The Elder looks into Yehuda's eyes.

71

"Please," Yehuda says once again to his own wonder. "Please find a way to forgive him. To forgive us."

The Elder listens to the young man translate Yehuda's words, staring into the remnants of the Duma Mosque. He shakes his head slowly.

"*La'a*," says the elder.

"No," the young man translates.

"*Av'da*."

"Not ever."

Then with fierce resolve, the Elder turns and speaks to Yehuda in his own tongue.

"Now go."

The black chasm in the mountain seems to stare into the marrow of the old man and snicker. It is night. Yehuda stands once again upon this precipice, without his goat, without Avram and perhaps even, he imagines, without God. His heart is Solomon's, beating frantically. His bride, a more insidious sort: the cave of Halamish.

Yehuda looks down at his hand. Gripped within his right fist is a short jagged rock, a crude knife he unearthed for protection. He tucks it into his pocket. Then Yehuda pulls up his left pant leg to check the bandage, now dirty and blood-soaked. He assumes the stitches ripped in his hurried hike to the cave of the sikrikim.

Groaning, Yehuda lifts the foot, swings it forward and places it before him. He takes one step into the chasm. Then another. And soon Yehuda finds himself descending the black innards of the mountain at a rapid pace. Above him, he discerns sharp limestone stalactites. Beneath him, jagged rock and sand.

After ten minutes of steep descent, Yehuda slows his pace. The passageway before him severs into two. One ingression leads deeper into the abyss without a curvature in the rock. The other, smaller path juts out right and snakes into an indiscernible dark.

These sikrikim are still boys, Yehuda thinks. They *will not dig in deeper.*

Yehuda advances toward the latter path. He winds along its many crooks and corners, watching his feet carefully.

Minutes pass. Yehuda knows not how many. The path grows into a slim sandstone tunnel. Yehuda sucks in his stomach and presses his face to the wall, attempting to slide through. The tunnel floor grows more sharp-toothed; he feels an edge scrape against his ankle.

Could Yehuda curse, he would this punishing stone.

He groans but pushes forward. After a few more precarious steps, Yehuda begins to second-guess his choice and gazes back longingly at the cave's entrance. He takes another step forward and, surprised by the ease of this motion, the old man halts his momentum. His legs are free. Soon his whole body plunges out of the sandstone corridor and Yehuda spins his head forward to see he now stands within a colossal grotto.

What strikes Yehuda first is the towering ceiling and the vastness of the space. But then he finds a more significant feature: an endless array of passageways along the grotto's walls. They are each a potential refuge, each a gaping mouth mocking Yehuda's pursuit of the sikrikim.

Chagrin becomes fury becomes despair and it stirs within his gut, rises into his throat, and eventuates into an unhinged howl. He is about to release the sound, when a faint light catches his eye. Yehuda throws his hands to his lips and holds them there, repressing the noise just in time.

At the opposite side of the grotto, Yehuda perceives the glowing embers of a dying campfire. He stands very still and attempts to quiet his breathing. He releases his hands from his face and focuses his eyes upon the distant figures beside the logs and charcoal.

Yehuda cannot be sure, but through the dim he discerns four young slumbering men. He tiptoes gingerly toward them, eyeing the ground with great caution. One loose stone, one snapped twig, the ruffling of his khaki pants—any sound could rouse them.

He remains patient, leading his legs forward at a glacial pace. He sees more clearly now. They are each wrapped in a dirty blanket. Scattered about are empty cans of corn and chicken feathers and greasy bones.

A small wooden shelf, rather novel in the setting, leans against the grotto wall. Upon its shelves lie ritual articles as familiar to Yehuda as the lines upon his old palms. Holy books and long-fringed garments and leather teffilin. And beside the shelf, among these holy items, sits an old wooden rifle. Loaded.

Yehuda steps so close to the campfire now, he can almost distinguish the face of one of the boys. He bends down to stare into the youth's face. Blonde and prepubescent and covered in dirt. The boy scowls, ferocious even in his slumber.

Yehuda rises and glances at the other three shapes. *Avram,* he thinks, *where do you hide?*

He squints around the campfire and notices a fifth blanket without an occupant. His eyes suddenly turn from slits into two pale ovals as the meaning dawns upon him.

Footsteps. He hears the legs approaching and he stands stiff. There is no time to hide. Nowhere to flee. He turns his face toward the sound and sees a teenager emerge from one of the grotto's passageways, a roll of toilet paper in his hand and a rifle strapped over his shoulder. The guard takes a step toward the campfire, his eyes fixed lazily to the grotto floor. Then he raises his head.

Eyes meet eyes. Both the young sentinel and the old man stand very still. The boy's hand creeps toward the stock of his rifle. The old man extends his splayed hand toward the teenager in supplication. The boy lips unfurl.

"Guys…" the boy tries, holding his breath.

He glances down at the motionless blankets.

"Guys!" he yells. "Wake up!"

The whole grotto reverberates with the sound of the guard's voice and in the same instant, the boys jump to their feet, spot the old intruder and point their various weapons in his direction.

"Who are you?!" the guard shouts out.

"How did you find us?" asks another.

The blonde steps toward Yehuda, rifle in hand. "Let's kill him," he says, advancing.

Then a calm voice, a voice Yehuda knows, rings out and quiets the others and halts the fair-haired boy where he stands.

"And if he be an angel?"

Yehuda stares at the source of these words, at a face draped in shadow and the small, sharp, shining teeth revealed in his allocution. No, it is not Avram, but Yehuda knows the stranger still.

"He doesn't look like an angel to me," says the blonde.

Now the stranger steps forward, closer to the embers of the campfire and Yehuda sees the light shine in those dark beady eyes, which flick back and forth.

"Friend," he says to the blonde, "do not mistake the appearance for the essence of a man."

And now Yehuda remembers and a sudden tremor seizes his every limb.

"You will be..." the speaker says, "disappointed."

"Zohar," Yehuda whispers, as if the word were hallowed.

The other boys gaze back and forth from the old man to the once Yeshiva student.

"You know him, Zohar?" the sentinel asks.

"Yes," Zohar says. "We were briefly acquainted...once."

"Son, listen to me," Yehuda says, his voice rasping. "All I seek is Avram."

Zohar strides along the grotto floor from boy to boy, lowering their weapons. The gun, then the saber, then the other rifle, each descends.

"Zohar," Yehuda repeats, "do you hear me?"

"How did you come here?" he asks as he touches the blonde's hand gently.

"Kahan once spoke of this place," Yehuda says. "He called you *hasmoneans*."

"Ah, but we have many appellations," Zohar says, eyeing the ceiling of the grotto.

"Yes," Yehuda nods. "Yes, Zohar. The Arabs call you djinns."

"So you have witnessed our endeavors?"

"Your profanities, yes. Your desecrations."

Zohar's eyes dart toward the old man and ignite, for the briefest second, in rabid fury. Then, just as quickly, the boy reconstructs his mien into an innocuous frown and feigns indifference. This flurry of caprice does not pass unnoticed by Yehuda.

"*But if you do not drive out the inhabitants of the land,*" Zohar recites, gazing out into the ether of the grotto, "*those you allow to remain will become barbs in your eyes and thorns in your sides.*"

Zohar turns his face toward Yehuda. "It is a mitzvah to kill the *amalekite*," he says. "Or have you forgotten?"

"You suggest these Arabs, whose sanctuary you pillage, are their spiritual heir?"

"I do not suggest," Zohar says. "I do not imply. I act, as the willing hand of God."

"And who, Zohar," Yehuda asks, bearing his cement teeth, "who appointed you?"

Zohar smirks. "Yehuda," he says. "I know what you are."

Now the boy strides toward Yehuda slowly.

"The day we met in Nahliel, I read you like a book, old man. I sought and soon discovered your...shortcomings."

Yehuda's posture stiffens.

"Yes," Zohar says. "You imitate true belief, you spin silver with that marvelous tongue of yours, but I know you for what you are, apostate."

And now, only a meter away, Zohar whispers into Yehuda's ear his infernal venom.

"God is, to you, a myth, is he not, Yehuda?"

"Arrogant devil!" Yehuda cries out. "You know nothing!"

"Nothing?!" Zohar shouts and now those eyes are mad with delight. "You picked that cretin Avram over me, not faulting my insight of the book but terrified by my insight into you. I could see the doubt fermenting within you like a sickness, see how it ate away at your sanity. Even now, I see it there."

Yehuda shakes his head.

"No," he says as firmly as he can muster, "I believe."

"Ha!" Zohar cries. "You are a mere result of your instruction. Like all *haredim*. Nothing more."

"And what are you, boy?" Yehuda asks under his breath.

Zohar tilts his head back, peering into the grotto's stalactites.

"What am I?" he asks the ceiling. "I, who raided the Judean landscape like the *kanai'im* of old? I, whose faith has burned the sanctuaries of amalekites to ashes?"

He slides toward the young blonde boy and grabs him by the back of his neck.

"I, who have heard the Lord whisper into my ear, have heard his decrees in the desert wind? I…"

Zohar turns his possessed eyes to Yehuda and whispers.

"I am the Lord's agent."

Yehuda trembles in disbelief.

"Child," he says, "you are mad. Mad and nothing more."

Zohar does not move a muscle but the effort he exerts to appear unmoved reveals itself in the recesses of his hysterical eyes.

"Zohar," Yehuda mutters, quieting his voice. "Tell me, where is Avram?"

"What does it matter?" asks Zohar.

"He is my boy."

"Do not lie," the boy says, snorting. "Avram was merely your tool."

Dimwits do make the best mules. Yehuda remembers his callous disregard of the boy and shudders.

"Zohar, please," Yehuda says wearily. "It is all I ask. Avram was here. What happened to him?"

Zohar turns to his disciples and waves a hand toward their weapons. Then he looks back into Yehuda's eyes, approaches him slowly and speaks without the slightest sentiment.

"Avram is dead, Yehuda."

The boys behind Zohar raise their weapons, steering their barrels and blades toward the old man. Their leader turns to address his disciples.

"He is not an angel, after all," Zohar tells them. "Make one of him."

Yehuda does not hesitate. As two of the boys, the blonde and the guard, cock their rifles, Yehuda's hand slithers into his pocket to grasp the jagged rock. With his other hand, Yehuda seizes Zohar by the nape of his neck and pulls him to his chest. Then he thrusts the crude blade against the boy's throat.

"I'll kill him!" Yehuda bellows, his bloodshot eyes bulging.

Zohar shrieks in fright and the boys stare at one other, astonished.

"I swear, I will kill your shepherd where he stands!" Yehuda screams, spittle dribbling down his rotten teeth. "Throw the guns away!"

Three of the boys comply immediately, casting their weapons aside. The blonde boy, however, stands steadfast. He grips his rifle hard against his chest and glares at Yehuda. Yehuda considers the barrel aimed between his eyes and nods his head.

"Fine," he says.

He places the rock against Zohar's right cheek and pierces the skin with the edge. Zohar shrieks and lurches, but Yehuda holds the boy steady. He pulls the edge up Zohar's face, carving a long crooked gash.

"Stop!" Zohar screams. "Please!"

The blonde boy, horror-struck, throws the rifle to the ground. Yehuda points all four of Zohar's disciples toward a passageway behind the camp-fire. "Go," he says, "or he dies."

Without pause, each boy turns around and descends into the passage-way. Yehuda waits until they are one with the dark and then he wrenches Zohar backward, knife to throat. He lugs the whimpering boy across the grotto, his eyes glued to the passageway. The disciples remain enshrouded in the shadows.

At last, Yehuda and his captive arrive at the thin corridor and the old man pushes Zohar through. Together, they cross the winding limestone path, arrive at the rupture of the two passageways, and climb the jagged stones toward the chasm above, through which the infinite stars gleam.

At the top, the two men finally withdraw from the cave. Yehuda exhales long rattling breaths and fills his lungs with the cool air of the mountain-side. He throws Zohar to the rocky floor and bends over, gasping. Never has Yehuda summoned such force. He looks down at the boy's bleeding face, full of tears and, for a moment, he pities him.

But then Yehuda remembers. *Avram is dead.* He knows no more com-passion, no clemency. He bends down to Zohar's face, places the jagged rock against the boy's unscathed cheek, slashes it fast and shrieks.

"Why?! Why did you kill him?!"

Zohar grips his face, gasps, and hyperventilates. Yehuda slaps him across the face, smeared with blood.

"Why, boy?! Tell me!"

"We—" Zohar tries. "We did not kill Avram."

"What? But you said—"

"Dead," the boy nods. "Yes. But not by our hand."

"Then who?"

Zohar hesitates, blinks his beady black eyes and then slowly shapes his mouth into a warped shaking grin.

"The God you deny," he says.

Yehuda thrusts the knife against the boy's throat.

"Tell me what happened," he says, nearly growling.

Blood seeps down into Zohar's gaping mouth, upon his small pointed teeth, and Yehuda thinks of the jackals.

"Okay," Zohar says slowly. "On our way back from the village, your boy, he…"

And now, to Yehuda's amazement, Zohar begins to giggle.

"He cried!" Zohar exclaims, amused. "He clasped his hands together and looked up into the heavens and begged forgiveness! The fool!"

Zohar grips his sides as if he's never heard a yarn so rich. Yehuda, as he hears these words, feels the cavity between his ribs fill with a dull throbbing ache. He thinks of Avram, of the incorrigible goodness that remained within him even then at the end of his fleeting life, and he loves the boy. He loves his young friend as he loved nothing his whole bitter life.

Yehuda lifts his eyes to the dark sky above and appeals in a silent prayer. *Whatever celestial face you take,* he thinks, *whatever grand ambitions you harbor, if you exist, Lord, I beg you. Shelter Avram as I failed.*

Yehuda drops his face into his trembling hands and then, between his interlocked fingers, he addresses Zohar.

"How…how did he die then?" Yehuda asks.

"Avram?" Zohar asks with indifference. "The imbecile collapsed there on his knees, blubbering and reciting the kaddish. We told him to shut up, but he would not. He refused to budge, so we left him in the desert. I no longer needed him. He became useless the minute he let his sympathies for the amalekites overcome him. Just like Saul before him, for this he was punished by God. We watched his speck from a kilometer away and saw him fall face-first into the dust."

Yehuda lowers his hands from his face. He does not meet Zohar's eyes. Instead he stands and contemplates the wilderness before him within a mournful hush. A few minutes of stifling silence pass and then Zohar re-awakens.

"God took him from you," the boy tells Yehuda. "God took everything from you. And yet, you are not Job. This is no test. This is the price you pay for your treacherous disbelief."

Yehuda nods his head.

"Within your words, Zohar," Yehuda says, "there may be some semblance of truth. But just as I am no Job, you are no prophet. And a day will come, when the false deity who chatters in your ear reveals itself to you as the product of your lunacy and hubris and nothing more."

Yehuda throws the makeshift knife among the other rocks. Zohar flinches.

"You, Zohar, will be as godless as I."

On the mountainside of Halamish, beside the entrance to the cave of the sikrikim, the old man bends down upon his knees and grabs the boy's bloody face in two clenched hands. He pulls the boy's ear to his lips and he whispers into the ear a curse.

Yehuda rises while Zohar shrieks in terror. The old man turns around and hobbles away from the wretched boy and the chasm in the mountain.

"Goodbye Zohar," Yehuda says under his breath. "Do not grieve, for we are both doomed men."

B'nei Eli and its creator face one another again. Yehuda, his suit in tatters, his skin caked in coats of dirt, his left leg limp and bloody, stares awestruck at the tall mound of fresh sand. The stable where Rushka once dwelt, the leaning water tower, the rubble road and the small house Yehuda called home—they are mere fiction. Swallowed by the earth.

But am I Korah? Yehuda asks himself. *How have I betrayed you, Lord?*

The old man sways where he stands. He remembers the mefaked's forewarning and marvels at how long ago that day seems. To the site where his house once stood, Yehuda limps and, with a long acacia stick, Yehuda traces the house's outline in the sand.

Yehuda steps inside the invisible edifice and lowers himself to the ground, the sand his floorboards and the sun his ceiling. He turns his head to examine the dust for some residuum of his existence. Some discarded page of a book, some rusty nail or thread of a rug. But the mountaintop is barren.

Yehuda shuts his eyes to veil the sunlight, to deaden the sun's eternal exigency for a moment so that all might be as meaningless as he. He feels the heat creep along his tucked eyelids, relentless, and moans in agony.

Stripped of ambition and faith and the little love he possessed, what is Yehuda? What is he who owns and knows and loves nothing?

The God Yehuda devoted his entire life to worship, despite the torment of repressing his doubt, the God he persecuted others in the name of and for whom he spurned his own home and brothers, this God, this great con the world calls God, is to Yehdua the real traitor.

He yearns to curse him, but innate superstition still muzzles his mouth.

"So be it!" he shrieks, and now he rises to his knees and spins his head around the empty horizon, seeking. "You desert me, and I, you!"

He rises to his feet and twists and pivots and whirls about in circles.

"You win!" he bellows into the wind. "I am but a shell! My only home, these bones. Are you contented? Tell me! If you be, then speak!"

The desert wind howls.

"Speak!" Yehuda shouts.

As the old man's voice reverberates across B'nei Eli's summit, beneath his feet he suddenly feels an erratic rumbling. He hears a low hum, senses the advent of some familiar force. His eyes bulge out of their sockets.

The drone, steadily rising in volume, resounds across the hills of Shilo, accompanied now by other stranger sounds. Metallic gasps and rumbling weight. Yehuda squints into the distance and sees a black spot rise upon the mountainside.

First, out of the blur, the machine gun takes shape, then the spinning tires and then the whole mud-caked frame of the fast approaching military Hummer. Yehuda bows down his head in mortification. *Soldiers,* he thinks. *Just soldiers.*

The Hummer speeds along the rocky terrain and, thirty meters away from Yehuda, it slides to a halt. The engine quiets, the passenger doors fly open and three soldiers pour out. They are strangers to Yehuda, adorned with black boots and gaudy pins. One of them, wearing three blue stripes upon his sleeves and thick, black eyebrows on top his eyes, approaches Yehuda.

"Sir," says the new mefaked. "You are Yehuda, right?"

Yehuda does not move a muscle.

"Well," the mefaked says, "somebody called and reported a homeless man hobbling along Highway 433. But when we figured out your destination, we, eh…"

He scratches the back of his head. "We put the pieces together."

Yehuda stares into the mefaked's eyebrows and, for once, he hushes all his judgments.

"Yehuda," the mefaked continues. "Two days ago at oh-eight-fifteen hours, twelve illegal outposts within the West Bank were simultaneously razed to the ground by the Combat Engineer unit. These orders came directly from the IDF Lieutenant General."

Yehuda bores his eyes into the ground.

"Your outpost, Yehuda," the mefaked says, "was one of these twelve. All of your personal belongings were temporarily stored with Shvut Rachel security. They said they know you there. A man named Baruch vouched for you."

The mefaked hesitates, trying to read the old man's countenance.

"We could give you a ride there if you like," the mefaked offers.

Yehuda shakes his head vehemently.

"You're sure? It's no—"

"Yes," Yehuda finally croaks. "Yes, I am sure. No thank you."

The mefaked's thick eyebrows pile up over his nose. "That's odd," he says, frowning. "You're courteous. They said—"

"What they said was true," Yehuda interrupts. "I am a psychotic old man. No more."

The mefaked shakes his head slowly.

"Avram doesn't speak of you this way," he says. "He—"

The words dissolve in the mefaked's mouth at the sight of the trauma and awe plastered across the old man's face.

"What was that?" Yehuda asks, his pitch high and breathy.

"I…" the mefaked stammers, "I said that your friend, Avram…the boy in the outpost near Kohav HaShahar, he spoke of you warmly."

"Avram is dead," Yehuda says.

"No, sir. We visited him yesterday on our patrol."

Yehuda gapes at the mefaked, uncertain if what his eyes behold is a mirage, if what his ears hear is merely an old mind's delirium.

"Say it again," he says. "Say the boy is alive."

"He is alive, Yehuda," the mefaked says. "Why would you think otherwise?"

Yehuda shuts his eyes to desist the seductive whispering within his heart, to quiet this cruel hope. He opens them, watering, and raises his gaze toward the mefaked.

"Will you take me there?" he asks.

One of the soldiers from behind pipes up.

"Too far," he says. "No way."

The other expresses his disquiet.

"You heard what the old unit said about this guy! I mean, look at him! He's nuts!"

Yehuda nods his head and bores his eyes into the ground. The mefaked watches him, scrunches his heavy eyebrows as if trying to resolve some impossible conundrum.

"Yehuda," he says, "can we trust you?"

The two soldiers gawk at one another in disbelief. Yehuda raises his eyes to meet the mefaked's and, with dignified equanimity, he nods his head.

"Good," the mefaked says. "Then follow me."

Beneath the roar of the hummer's engine, the old man's ears detect the sound of dogs barking. He gazes out the muddy window and perceives a short house, reminiscent of his own but gawkier, and a series of other primitive buildings overrunning the desolate landscape.

The Hummer comes to a halt and Yehuda's hand scrambles to turn the handle and throw open the passenger door and propel himself out of the vehicle. Before him, a German Shepherd and an ugly mutt lean down on their haunches, baring their teeth and barking at the old man. Yehuda ambles forward, oblivious.

"Avram!" he shouts out, eyes scanning the horizon.

The main house's door flies open and a Yemenite boy, maybe eighteen years old, strides out, bracing an iron shovel. Yehuda stalls.

"What are you doing here?" the boy asks, addressing the soldiers exiting the Hummer.

"Relax, Shimi," the mefaked says. "We're just reuniting Yehuda here with his friend."

"What friend?"

"Avram."

The Yemenite boy, this Shimi, stops in his tracks and eyes Yehuda with naked contempt.

"You…" he says incredulously, "you are Avram's friend?"

Yehuda smiles. "He is here then?"

"You're too old to be his friend."

Yehuda opens his mouth to respond and shuts it. The Yemenite boy's presumptions and condescension strike Yehuda as reminiscent of none other than himself. A prior self.

"Please," Yehuda says and now it slips off his lips as fluidly as a recollected prayer. "Please, I just want to see my old pupil."

Taken aback by the oppressive modesty of the old stranger and his alleged rapport with Avram, Shimi frowns and shrugs.

"Avram is in the barn," he says. "Make it quick."

Then Shimi whistles to the dogs. "Come on boys," he says, turning back toward the house. "Follow me."

The dogs follow their master obediently and Yehuda, watching the dumb animals chase him with their wagging tails, sees how a man—regardless of his true worth—might gain the world's influence without ever earning it.

Yehuda turns away and sets off toward the wooden barn behind the house. Drawing near the barn doors, Yehuda slows his pace. He places his cheek to the splintering wooden wall and listens. Within he hears the sounds of toil and the huffing and grunting of an all too familiar voice. Yehuda retreats a step, inhales slowly and then pushes open the door.

"Avram?" he asks the shadows.

The red boots he notices first. They take a step into the sunlight. Then the ripped T-shirt and shorts akin to rags, move toward him. Last, the sweaty arms as they spring forward and wrap around the old man's neck.

"Yehuda!" Avram cries. "You found me!"

At the sound of the boy's voice, Yehuda collapses onto his knees and embraces the boy by his abdomen.

"Avram!" he cries out. "You're alive!"

"Of course I am," Avram says, gasping.

He tries to pry the old man's arms off of him.

"Yehuda," he says, "calm down. I'm fine."

Yehuda rises to his feet and touches the boy's cheeks as if to ensure their authenticity. He stares into the blue of Avram's eyes and sees they are the same, but changed. Darker.

"You are…" Yehuda says. "You are fine."

"Yes, Yehuda," Avram says, shaking his head. "Come now."

Avram takes Yehuda's arm in the crook of his elbow and leads the old man out of the barn toward the rocky trail that encircles the settlement. Together at last, the two men slowly wend their way around the border.

For a long while, neither man speaks; they simply walk along, reveling in their odd reconciliation. Then after a few minutes, Avram abruptly drops Yehuda's arm and spins to face him.

"I'm sorry," Avram blurt outs.

Yehuda does not meet the boy's eyes.

"I am sorry I left you there, alone," Avram continues. "I didn't know you would go looking for me. But, Yehuda…look at you!"

The boy gestures toward the old man's shredded clothes; his peeling skin and limping leg.

"What happened to you?" Avram asks.

Yehuda keeps his eyes fixed upon the horizon.

"Nothing of consequence," he says. "And do not ever apologize again, Avram. Not to me."

"No," Avram says. "You are my teacher! And I abandoned you! You must forgive me."

"Avram," Yehuda says curtly, "I will not say it again. You are forbidden to beg my forgiveness."

"But I must! After everything you taught me—"

"Lies," Yehuda interrupts. "The delusions of a decrepit, arrogant mind. The mere whims of a tyrant."

"No!" Avram shouts with such urgency, Yehuda turns to meet the boy's strange steely gaze.

"No," Avram says. "Whatever I am, Yehuda, I owe to you."

Avram deflates suddenly. "Oh, how selfish I have been!"

He glances down at his hands as they fidget with the fringes of his white under-shawl.

"The night I left B'nei Eli," he says, "I had heard these hesitations in your voice. I saw doubt in your eyes. It was so unlike you...I craved a change. And youth. Somebody confident."

Yehuda nods his head. "Zohar."

"Yes," Avram says, looking up. "You didn't know it, but Zohar and I were once friends in the Nahliel Yeshiva. And, long before you recruited me, Zohar had told me of his plans...so, when I left you, I went and found him."

"I know, Avram," Yehuda says. "I was there at the Duma village and in the caves of the sikrikim. I met your shepherd."

Avram scowls. "He is no shepherd of mine."

At these words, Yehuda feels the blood rush hot within his cheeks and he swells, simultaneously, with pride for the boy's inherent decency, and shame for the trim of his cobwebbed mind. He turns to accost Avram, but hesitates, noticing the boy's eyes wander.

"They left me alone in the desert," Avram says to the wind. "They left me there to die, discarded me like a piece of trash."

Avram gestures toward the house in the settlement's center.

"I'd be dead, were it not for Shimi," he says. "He found me out there and took me in. When I woke up, we spoke and he agreed to let me stay here as long as I'd work. I began two days ago and…I've been here ever since."

Yehuda nods and allows one last minute of quiet solitude to pass between them as they walk along the trail's bend. He cherishes this fleeting peace between them, but realizes with prescient regret, that he, Yehuda, must be the one to end it. He opens his mouth.

"Avram," he says, his voice shaking. "Listen to me and listen closely. I have come here, come to your new settlement to admit the truth, a truth you deserve to know. Listen to me, Avram…"

Yehuda looks into Avram's eyes and steadies the tremble of his throat.

"I am a fraud," he says.

At this, Avram frowns and opens his mouth to retort.

"No," Yehuda says, raising his hand. "Let me finish."

Avram acquiesces, reluctantly closing his lips.

"I never believed," Yehuda says. "I followed the mitzvot, I devoted my every waking moment to studying the Torah, I quoted the scripture and defined my life by ritual, yet the Almighty remained, within my heart, a stranger."

Avram's face drains of color. Yehuda continues.

"Faith was a sham, so long preserved, I began to believe my own fabrications. But then…when you left me in B'nei Eli…"

Yehuda's feet come to a halt. Avram too slows to a standstill, watching his old teacher with dawning apprehension.

"It all fell apart," Yehuda says quietly.

His eyes begin to swim. With a sharp intake of air, Yehuda holds the tears at bay.

"But these days in the desert," he says, "I watched the world around me change. I lost everything, even you. At last, the confession of my doubt fled my lips and I challenged God to prove me wrong."

Tears cascade down the old man's face and his grey teeth frame an indebted smile.

"The Lord answered me, Avram. He answers me now, revealing himself to me in you, in your every passing breath! I thought you dead—but here you are, resurrected, and for the first time in my life, I believe! My time in the desert, the meaning of my futile pursuits and my failures…it all becomes clear."

"Stop Yehuda," Avram says under his breath, staring at the desert floor.

"Listen to me, Avram," Yehuda says. "My crimes—I see them clearly now and I see that the very worst were inflicted upon you."

Yehuda places his trembling hand upon the boy's shoulder.

"All that I taught you was false," Yehuda says.

Now the old man hesitates. He opens his mouth, he attempts to speak but chokes. He cannot articulate the extent of his epiphanies—it is all too fresh and foreign and terrifying to impart. Avram shakes his head and, attempting to usurp the moment, he grazes Yehuda's wet cheek with his knuckles.

"Yehuda," he says, "you are weary. You are injured. Come."

Avram brings his hand to the old man's shoulder and gently pulls him. "We can talk later."

"No," Yehuda says under his breath. "No. I have something to say."

"Later," Avram says.

"No, it must be now!"

The old man freezes, his face resolute yet horribly agitated.

"You must listen, Avram," he says. "The sikrikim, they are wrong. The literal reading, it is...it is dangerous."

"Yehuda," Avram says, shaking his head. "I don't understand you."

"You see it yourself!" Avram exclaims. "Why else do you renounce Zohar and his minions?"

"I see what, Yehuda?"

"That God does not hunger for such savagery! The Torah is a book of metaphor!"

At this, Avram pulls his hand away from his old teacher and turns his body to face the desert.

"Enough, Yehuda," he mutters.

Yehuda lets fall his outstretched arm but presses on.

"I preached to you day in and day out, Avram, with such...such assurance. But what did I really know?"

Yehuda steps into the boy's field of vision, forcing him to meet his weeping eyes.

"I plead to you now," he says. "You must unlearn."

"Un-what?" Avram asks.

"Unlearn it all, Avram," Yehuda says, wiping his face, becoming serious. "You must forget the predetermined judgments, ask the questions I forbid you to consider. Go! Go and reopen the book of Bereishit with the unmarred eyes of a child. You will discover..."

Yehuda's mouth goes numb, his eyes grow wide, his entire countenance ensorcelled by this fresh revelation.

"You will discover," he repeats slowly, "what I, my whole life, missed. Avram, we are meant..."

Yehuda closes his eyes and breathes heavily.

"...to treasure the moral. Not the ritual."

As Yehuda's eyes open and peer into those of Avram, for once the old man sees that he cannot read them. Is it envy or pity, denial or acceptance, love or hatred he sees stirring within the stare of his former pupil. And then the boy opens his mouth.

"Heresy," Avram whispers.

"What?" Yehuda asks, aghast. "Avram, did you not—"

"The wilderness has made you mad, old man."

"No!" Yehuda says, shaking his head. "The opposite!"

"You…" Avram trails off, muttering. "You speak now like the Jews of Shvut Rachel, who you called imposters!"

"Yes!" Yehuda cries. "For they knew better than I. What we have read and accepted word for word was meant to be interpreted, Avram. The Torah—"

"Do not speak of the Torah!" Avram screams. "Enough!"

"Avram," Yehuda tries. "I—"

"No."

Avram shakes his head in disgust.

"You are demented, old man," he says. "You always were."

Yehuda feels a bloom of dread within his stomach.

"Avram," he says. "Please. I beg you. Let me help you. Let us unlearn together."

"You have done enough," Avram says coldly. "I am grateful for your education, Yehuda, but now you must go."

Avram turns his eyes away, fixes them upon the distant cypress trees of Jordan and Yehuda feels his heart pulse in the hollow of his throat. He understands that his young apprentice from B'nei Eli is gone. Zohar's lunacy, the flames of Duma, the desertion, Shimi's new influence—together they helped mold the boy into this rigid man. But no man inspired Avram as greatly as his old teacher, with his radical instruction and seductive vehemence. No man did more to transform Avram's eyes, once so weak and watery, into the frozen cold sinister pair they now resemble, than Yehuda himself.

Yehuda touches Avram's hand, expecting him to flinch, but the boy is still.

"Go and see your family," Yehuda says. "Regardless of your convictions, they love you."

"Then they are weak," Avram mutters, though the words appear to pain him.

Yehuda takes a step toward him and with his eyes, somehow sorrowful and buoyant, he appraises the young man one last time. He kisses Avram's cheek and leans toward his ear.

"If I could change," Yehuda says, "then for you, there is still hope. Goodbye, son."

Avram remains very still, his eyes fixed upon the Jordanian countryside. He yearns to turn his head, to watch his old teacher go but pride, that devil, restrains him.

When he is certain the old man must be distant, Avram turns around. His eyes inspect every corner of the mountain crest, hovering momentarily on a pair of rolling tumbleweeds and on an outburst of malaki rock. Still, Avram finds no vestige of the old man, as if Yehuda consorted with the wind and, crumbling, took flight within the desert breeze.

He approaches the house at the center of the settlement and sees the soldiers, beside their Hummer, smoking cigarettes.

"Hey!" Avram yells out. "Hey! Where did Yehuda go?"

Avram runs up to the mefaked.

"What'd you say?" the mefaked asks.

"Yehuda—" Avram says, "did you see which way he walked?"

The mefaked shakes his head, furrowing his immense eyebrows. "He was with you, I thought."

Avram looks out at the horizon, blue eyes flicking back and forth in pursuit of the old man. But deep inside he knows Judea to be a ravenous desert, swallowing men whole without compunction. This land where the outlaw and the settler rule; where the soldier buzzes about in cyclical impotence; where the Arab conspires and the Bedouin watches, indifferent.

Yehuda is one with this wilderness now, faded into its infinite dust. For a brief moment, Avram mourns the old man, madness and all. But as the mefaked touches his shoulder and rouses him from his bereft reverie, Avram decides there is no time to grieve. No room in his life for the past. All Avram knows is his purpose.

"Avram," the mefaked says, shaking his shoulder. "Where is Yehuda?"

"I do not know," says Avram.

"Aren't you worried?"

Avram tsks and turns to consider the mefaked with contempt.

"What do you care?"

"I'm just saying—"

"It is of no interest to me," Avram says. "Now, get out of here."

The mefaked looks at Avram, amazed.

"You should be grateful, kid," he says, screwing up his eyebrows.

"Why?" Avram asks.

"One day," he says, waving his hand toward the settlement's structures, "we will come back here with orders to rip down this outpost. And you will have to sit there and watch as we tear every building to the ground."

Avram grunts to indicate his incredulity.

"I'd like to see you try," he says.

The mefaked stares into the boy's cold eyes as if he'd never discerned them before and shakes his head.

"You crazy religious," the mefaked mutters.

He calls his soldiers, they stamp out their cigarettes and all three men pile into the muddy Hummer, slamming their car doors shut. The engine starts with a roar, the tires turn, spitting back rubble, and the army hummer flies off into the distance toward Shilo.

Avram watches it go, gazes around at his settlement-to-be and lifts his blue eyes up to peer into the darkening sky.

Praise God, the boy whispers to himself.

And then he spits into the sand.

BY THE LAMP POST

Every morning at 2 A.M., when the guard shift switches and Gal relinquishes his post to the next depressed host, he slogs alone through the concrete fortress, heading toward the soldiers' quarters, toward his blessed bed where at last he rests.

Every morning at 2 A.M., when the Intel. Branch empties and Yarden signs the final entries, she scrambles across the metal complex, following spray paint directions, peering through the fog, the gloom, for a sign of her room.

And every morning at 2:08, give or take a minute,

Gal and Yarden are simultaneously illuminated by an iron lamp post.

At most ten feet high, the pole carries a pinkish light, its plastic cover colored in with a red felt-tip marker to further darken the base, further obfuscate the trace of any operations along the border, to keep away the eyes of Mordor.

And through this red-penned light, each sees another existence ignite.

As she watches Gal materialize, become a man out of a vague shade, cutting forward through the fog like a mad freight train, Yarden wonders if—maybe craves that it be him.

Is it the one who always wears the pair of bags beneath his eyes?

In that weary stare hides an elegance; Yarden swears she can see it, sense the stranger's brimming life.

Gal tries to conceal it. He tries all but to reveal how she makes that which was always dormant wake in him—an ache. He pries his eyes away from her to stare instead at the fog-stained sky.

So it is every night.

Despite how time and fate have seemed to contrive their meeting on this path of sand-bags and metal sheeting, Gal and Yarden remain strangers—that is—until tonight.

Blind, neither Gal nor Yarden can find the light they've so long relied upon without question.

That which had burned in its pink incandescence burned out, leaving the route enveloped in a dim and its inhabitants within without the slightest doubt: bound they were tonight to meet.

To speak! To dare let dreams crumble so that which is real might breathe— and as Gal's steps bring him closer to the threshold once-seen, his nerves find their voice and they mumble their creed:

Might he have already assembled a series of flawless impossibles no real girl could rival?

Thus fear makes him freeze.

Yarden shares not this envy of her dreams.

Instead she teems with stray impulses. All their cowardly choices inevitably led toward this: this, the face to face, no holds barred engagement. Let the quiet be damned, tear apart their estrangement—so darkness does implore these amorous forces to come forth.

When each reaches the lamp post's cover, both slow their pace. Gal even tiptoes.

Sees the faint contour of each the other but how fog smothers the space.

Yarden waits no longer. She asks, "Hello?" Her greeting meets silence.

"I know you hear me," she says. But whatever his reasons, Gal remains quiet.

She treads toward his figure, this faint silhouette, and sees a flash then flicker.

He lights a cigarette.

Gal makes sure to glue his eyes to the ember, to remember that what he loves in her is what he loves in all strangers, the dreaming nature with which others they behold.

To awaken her to him is to forsake all foretold could-have-beens.

He drags the tobacco thin

and Yarden feels less bold.

As her foot finds its hold a centimeter away from his mud-stained boot, leaving in between the two this still restrained mute, she balks. If this were a real meet-cute, she muses, already he'd have moved.

Then the wind shifts. Before Gal can reconsider, his eyes lift; they front hers like a pair of challenged hunters, and whatever blunders Gal might have made, they seem to Yarden as strange and foreign as the world's extinct wonders.

She stays her smile, pulls him forward, says: "For a warrior, you're a real coward."

And then she kisses him.

The lamp post never glows again.

THE WOLF-CRIERS

To this day, I blame the snow. Snow's got no business squatting on a hot little country like this.

The year was…no. Never mind the year. When don't make a damn difference. Just know the where: a mountain by the name of Har Dov, a black swollen pimple sitting aside the majestic whitehead, Mount Hermon. I served on top of that icy mound for six months—the six most charmed fucking months of my life. But lest I brood more than a sober Russian on Sylvester—meaning: New Year's—I'll try my best to sketch you a picture, detail the other guys I shared that frozen over hell with.

Levi, Fitness, Tooke, Berman, Mengisto, Udi, Schnitzer—to name a few. We were only surnames there, leaving our firsts for mommy and daddy and life off the catwalk. Nobody brought home back to base, unless they were itching to get bullied as bad as that idiot, Fitness. No, on Har Dov we ate shit and grinned all the while. That was the way of—what we called—the Warrior Code. When asked the difference between a kid and a man, we'd answer that when the kid suffers, he cries, but when the man suffers, he laughs. So in this way, we figured ourselves men. For a while.

"Give me your wafers," Udi said to Berman, voice filtered those loud asthmatic breaths of his.

We were lying on our cots one night, busy counting sheep in vain when this argument started, only memorable thanks to the shit that followed it.

"Eat your own wafers," Berman said, trying hard to roll his r's and camouflage that Jersey-bred drawl. No dice.

"Why are you such trash?" said Udi. "Just open the wafers."

99

"Never heard of, 'Please'?" asked Berman.

"Nope," said Udi, cracking a smirk. "Never heard of that 'Thank you' one either."

"What is it with you Israelis, always just expecting people to hand over their food and cigarettes, like you paid for them too?"

"Watch it," said Tooke from out of nowhere. "You want us to start on you Americans?"

They'd thought that Tooke was asleep. He had a real knack for that—bursting all chafed into the middle of a perfectly nice civilized row. Then came the ranting.

"Ah, damn it, Tooke," Berman said. "Why'd you have to wake up?"

"*Kus'emek*," Udi hissed under his breath—meaning: your mother's cunt—or in most cases: shit.

"Now, listen to me!" Tooke began. "You may call it chutzpah. You may call it rude and presumptuous. But the Israeli way is to share and I, for one, am proud that—"

"Anyway, Berman," Udi said. "Just save me a wafer for later."

"Sure, whatever," said Berman.

"What?" Tooke asked. "Is no one listening to me?"

"I am!"

That would be Fitness. He had a real name—some Ashkenazi shit with a Schtat or a Stein in it—don't remember. Point is, he was whiter than Wonder Bread and the sort of guy to eat it with the crusts cut off. We called him Fitness 'cause after every free weekend he brought a box of Fitness cereal back to base with him. We were pretty sure he was gay too, which didn't help.

"Really?" said Tooke, devastated. "Fitness is the only one that's listening?"

Fitness beamed at Tooke, all heart and comradery, which in turn shut Tooke the hell up. For this use alone, we cherished Fitness. Nobody, not even the most righteous of the *datim*—meaning: religious soldiers—could handle the kid's otherworldly goodness. It maddened the best of us. For when home was called Har Dov, no one had the right to be so damn sunny.

If memory serves me right, Levi opened the door at that point and entered our shipping container barrack.

"Listen up," he said. "We got an order. Everybody, be fully equipped by twelve sharp. Magazines, Camelbaks, rain-gear—the whole deal."

"What?!" said Udi. "Right now?"

"No, yesterday," Levi said, serious as cancer. How we detested him, our dwarf commander, our mefaked. Our hairy little runt. Never has Napolean complex been as rightly diagnosed as it was to Levi (by yours truly, I might add). A few weeks later, that *malamnik*—meaning: ass-kisser—would get shipped off to officer's school to become a *mem mem*, AKA officer.

Good riddance, if you ask me.

"Wait," started Mengisto, our platoon's token Ethiopian and probably my only real friend. "Are we going on a mission right now?"

"What does it sound like?" Levi said.

Then clearing his throat, Tooke said, "Well, if that's the case, I just want to say—"

"Again, twelve sharp," Levi broke in. "We'll do an ammo check before we go, so don't screw around."

He flew out of the room. The dust resettled. We took a look at each another and, much unlike us, kept our traps shut for maybe thirty seconds. Something like excitement, albeit the edgy, hesitant kind, settled in.

Then Fitness said, "Schnitzer, you sure are quiet."

"Yeah, Fitness," I said, "and you sure are a pain in the ass."

The no man's land between Israel and Lebanon, what we called the Blue Line, stretched far beyond our company's assignment. We watched over nine ugly kilometers, a place the enemy called Shebba Farms and we called Har Dov. Underneath this contested border lay thousands of twenty-something year-old land mines, trigger happy little fuckers just aching to blow. Tonight, one had gone off and that's why we found ourselves trudging through frozen powder a few clicks outside base. As for our early enthusiasm, it went the way of our socks and pants: soaked then frozen then cursed.

"This...is...bullshit!" Udi yelled out, in between big gulping breaths.

"Yeah," said Mengisto. "Why are we the ones getting sent out here?"

Mengisto was black, and I mean the color. The kid looked darker than tarmac and he stuck out in the snow like a black sheep in a herd of white. I might add that I never met anybody more sensitive to the cold than he.

"What is with you Israelis, always bitching and moaning?" asked Berman.

"May I remind you, sir," began Tooke, "that despite your broad generalizations, we—"

"Will you all just shut the hell up?!" Levi shouted.

Begrudgingly we complied and on we walked. After a while, Levi spotted an entry down in the trenches and signaled for us to line up behind him single-file. This was the closest you could get to the mines without going the way of all flesh. We tiptoed along gingerly then stopped. Somebody sniffed loud.

"You guys smell that?" Levi asked.

At first I didn't. Then a few paces further, my nose met the scent: something like overcooked meat. Burned bad. My eyes watered.

I said, "What the hell is that?"

"Smells familiar," said Berman.

"Yeah?" Udi asked Berman, "You've smelled cooked Arab before?"

We pressed on through the narrow trench until we hit the fence. Levi pulled Tooke toward him.

"Tooke," he said, "Use your scope."

Tooke snapped down the bipods on the rifle's front, sat it on the ledge facing the field, pulled the stock hard against his chest, and peered through the *li'or*—meaning: Land Warrior PVS-14 night vision scope.

"See anything?" Levi asked.

"Plenty," said Tooke. "There's Beaufort, a few Lebanese villages, the U.N. base—"

"I mean," Levi pressed, "do you see any sign that a mine went off?"

Scanning the horizon, Tooke answered, "No, not really. Everything looks like it's supposed to. Maybe what we heard was just the...the..."

"What is it, Tooke?" Levi said.

"What—what the hell is that?" Tooke said.

"What do you see?"

"It's a body, alright. Parts."

Levi's eyes widened. Turning fast, he grabbed the handset off my vest, checked the channel on the radio in its back pocket, blew twice into the mic and spoke: "Maccabi, Maccabi from Aleph One."

Levi reported a positive identification to Maccabi, our base's Communications Branch. All jargon aside, the gist was this: Terrorists tries to enter Israel. Terrorist is toast. I looked at the other guys and saw in their expressions a sudden giddy sort of agitation. The border had been quiet so long, we'd gotten comfortable. And bored. This news, we understood, was about to shake shit up. While Levi talked to Maccabi about further action, Tooke adjusted the focus on his gun's li'or.

"Maccabi," Levi continued. "Consider green alert. Received?"

"Wait," Tooke said.

"Received, Maccabi. Wake up everybody on base," Levi said, ignoring Tooke.

"Levi!"

"What, Tooke?"

"It's a body but…"

"But what?!"

"I don't think it's human."

"Move," Levi said, pushing Tooke aside. He grabbed the M-4 for himself and took a look through the li'or. A minute passed. Then another. The radio blared with activity, calling Aleph One again and again. Finally Levi stood up, thrust the gun into Tooke's arms, grabbed the handset and said: "Maccabi, Maccabi. False alarm."

Then he turned around and started walking the other way.

"Everybody after me," he said.

"Wait," Udi said. "What was it?!"

"Nothing," said Levi. "Don't worry about it. We're going back."

"I'll tell you what it was!" Berman said, grinning. "Tooke, did you see any animals around?"

"Just the usual," Tooke said.

"Some boars, right?"

"Maybe. Yeah."

Berman put his arm around Udi's shoulder.

"I'll tell you what that was, alright."

Then in English he said, "Boys, tonight you all smelled bacon."

After that, we were the joke of the company. Honk, honk, honk. Snort, snort, snort. Kosher puns. The works. They called us suckers, they called us retards, they called us a lot of shit. But nothing hurt too bad at first. We were the *tzairim* after all—meaning: newcomers/noobs/rookies/tenderfeet, take your pick. We understood that this was the ritual, like a hazing ceremony from one of those American fraternities, the stuff of movies—just with guns and less grinning. So, following the Warrior Code, we laughed no matter how bad it hurt.

Mostly, the older guys were mad because we'd woken them up in the middle of the night, alarms blasting, over a blown up hog. One of them, a wide guy, face covered in furious tufts of beard, pulled me aside the next day. He said, "You little shits cry wolf again and you'll be sorry." He might as well have growled it.

Later, I told Mengisto about it and he let out that throaty guffaw of his.

"What did you expect from the Beard?" he asked me, still laughing. "He hates all tzairim."

"Good point," I said. "Got a cigarette?"

"Just cause it's you," Mengisto replied and he meant it. Cigarettes were the only currency we had up there and the better the brand, the worse you felt for bumming one. In this case, I felt especially bad. Mengisto smoked nothing but Lucky Strikes, the best import around besides the Chesterfields Berman lugged back by the suitcase-full from his American vacations.

"Thanks, man," I said, lighting that precious death stick.

"Don't mention it," Mengisto said. "Now, do me a favor."

"Anything."

"I'm done with Har Dov. I want out."

"You and everybody's mother."

"No," he said, serious all of a sudden. "You don't get it. I can't stay here another second. I'm dying here."

This, I must admit, did not move me. I had heard this kind of chatter since my first week of basic. Mostly from that *bachyan*—meaning: crybaby—Udi. Banal as all hell. But Mengisto wasn't like Udi and a bachyan he was not. So I humored him.

"Okay," I said. "What do you need?"

"Shoot me. Break my arm. Hit me so hard, I forget my name. *Kus'emek.* I don't know, Schnitzer. I just can't keep doing this. I'm done being a *lochem.*"

Lochem, meaning: warrior.

"I know it's tough, man," I said, "but that's what we signed—"

"Yeah, yeah, yeah," he said. "That's what we signed up for. You think I don't know that?"

Sadness suits some people better than others. Mengisto, with his pearly white grin and husky chortle, was not one. It killed me to see the kid so morose.

"Okay, fine," I said. "What do you really want to do?"

He looked at me hard, his eye to mine for I don't know how long. Then he said, "Get me out off this fucking mountain, man. Whatever it takes."

I had to stop. I had to concentrate. Neither of which I was accustomed to. So instead of sneaking to the guard posts with my phone up my sleeve, instead of playing Tetris or Sudoku for those six-hour shifts, I daydreamed...how to get Mengisto off Har Dov?

There were plenty of methods but with each came some scary-ass outcome. The worst ended with me and/or Mengisto behind bars. The best: Mengisto behind a desk, typing or filing away. Some easy-peasy Japanesey job in the hot heart of *ha'aretz*—meaning: Israel. But how to get him there?

Then one night, scraping the frost off the windowsill at Guard Post Purple, it hit me. I'd get the kid sick. So damn sick, he'd turn white.

"I have a plan," I told him the next morning outside the kitchen, smoking another one of his Lucky Strikes. "And it's good. It'll work."

"Okay," he said. "What are you thinking?"

"Hold this," I handed him the cigarette and ran into the kitchen. When I came back out, I held a plastic bag full of ice.

"This, my friend, is your key so salvation!" I said.

"Eh?" he said.

"Very simple. Put this bag on your balls. Leave it there all night when you're on your six-hour shift at Guard Post Purple."

Mengisto opened his mouth to answer, looking a bit *b'shoke*—meaning: in shock, if you couldn't figure that out on your own.

"Let me finish," I said. "The idea is this: the ice will get you sick. I mean really sick. We're talking hypothermia, man…which is easily treated. There are plenty of paramedics around so it's not like you'll die!"

Mengisto's mouth still drooped there ajar.

"I know! It sounds crazy but it'll work, I'm telling you. You'll get a bunch of sick leave at least. And then, you just got to blame the irresponsibility of the army for throwing you into a guard post like Purple, where the windows are all broken and there's no heater. You'll get a trial, you'll win, and then you'll get the hell off Har Dov!"

Mengisto must have sat there gawking at me like a hungry pigeon for a full minute. Then finally his gaping mouth snapped shut and he spoke: "What are you, crazy?"

"I—" I started.

"It'll never work at the Purple Post," he said. "It's got to be Orange."

Given the choice, I would have forced Mengisto to go through with it that night. But it wasn't our platoon's turn to guard Orange. Purple and Yellow were our only assignments for the week. So I just told Mengisto: "Shut up, you Bachyan. Be patient. All you got to do is get through one more week here. That's it. Think about the Warrior Code."

He nodded. Then he handed me another Lucky Strike, a small expense for all my hard work. He stood up, took a last drag of his cigarette, flung the hot stub into the snow and said, "You know what, man? Fuck the Warrior Code." He walked away, the smoke fleeing his nostrils.

Kids cry, men laugh. So said the Code. But how in burning brimstone Christian hell do you know what a lochem does? Mengisto, I'm pretty sure, had it figured out; he knew what I only know now, too late and too pissed off. We were nothing but kids forced to grow up fast, wannabe men without the wisdom or the know-how. We talked and acted tough because that's what was called for. But the truth was there right in front of us, waving its gangly arms in a damn frenzy, trying to catch our attention: we were just kids. And, like kids, all we ached for was our mother's cooking.

This, I admit, took many years to sink in. As long as I froze my ass off on Har Dov, nothing but a faint wishy-washy idea, an abstract understanding existed of how fucked the Warrior Code really was. I followed it; I stood up for it because without the Code, I had zip. *Kus'emek.*

A few days after my talk with Mengisto, hiking on my merry way through a snowstorm to guard at Yellow, the Yiddish saying came true: Man plans, God laughs. God, that fiendish bastard, threw a wrench right into mine when the Comm. Branch's antenna exploded. Fifteen meters away from my face.

Right there in front of me, a blue mutant flame burst out mad and spectacular, blinding me; the force threw me to the floor. Sparks of every color soared out like confetti. Blood poured out of my useless ears. The floor shook—no, it rippled like a wave pool gone wild. I was, in a word, b'shoke.

What I remember: being wet. Being cold. Being deaf until I wasn't, 'til I heard somebody screaming, "War!" over and over and over, like a damn skipping record.

What I don't remember: I was wet because the rain kept pouring. Weather does not stop on war's behalf. And that madman screaming, "War!" was me.

Next thing I knew, Udi was above me, face contorted in fear. He dragged me across the catwalk, fast as he could, toward the guard post, toward cover. Whoever had shot the base, shot again. Udi dropped me and leapt away, hands over his head. The crack, the boom, it sounded loud, but from a distance. Must have hit the other side of the base. Udi, covered in mud and sand, scrambled back and pulled me toward him.

"Come on, man!" he screamed.

I could speak. I knew I could.

"Come on, Schnitzer! Talk to me!" he said.

"I hear you." I said.

"Good. Good. Kus'emek. What the—"

"Udi," I stopped him. "Listen!"

"Yeah, what?" he said, dragging me along.

"Leave me alone. Go sound the alarm."

"I'm sure they heard—"

"GO!" I yelled.

He got up and ran away with his head tucked down, almost between his knees. I saw him enter the cement post. I heard him sound the siren. I closed my eyes and then I breathed. Black.

When I came to, I was paralyzed. No, sorry—just tied down to a stretcher, being prodded, checked, double-checked, and talked to by some paramedic.

"Schnitzer!" he yelled. He slapped me in the face. Hard.

"Schnitzer! Can you hear me?!"

"Yeah," I said.

I looked to my left and to my right and saw green vests and bobbing helmets and overstuffed bags; I saw them running around, getting into formation. Everybody yelled. Everybody moved.

"Schnitzer!" the paramedic said. He grabbed my chin and forced me to face him. "Me! Pay attention to me."

"What's going on?" I asked.

"You're going down for treatment."

"Down, where?"

"Down to the city, off Har Dov."

Wheels started turning. Short-term memory roused.

"The bombs…" I said.

"No," said the paramedic. "Those weren't bombs. That was lightning, Schnitzer. It struck right next to you. You're lucky to be alive."

Lightning? I turned again to my left and saw the guys from my platoon, lining up. Levi checked their *konenut*—meaning: equipment and ammunition.

"So what's with the konenut check?" I asked.

"Procedure," the paramedic said, flicking the tip of a needle. "Somebody sounds the alarm, everyone follows it, drill or not. They're doing a war exercise next."

"What? Why?"

"*Mem pay* said so."

Mem pay, meaning: captain.

"The mem pay said that the whole company's response to your and Udi's alarm was way too slow."

I turned and saw the older guys with those massive bags on their backs, pissed as all hell and the Beard amongst them. He looked back right at me and shot me an exaggerated glare as if to say, "What did I tell you, tzair? You're dead!" I might as well have gulped.

"Ow!" I yelled out instead.

I turned to see a needle sticking out of me, shooting some clear liquid into my blood.

"Way to warn me," I told the paramedic.

He ignored the comment, finished tranquilizing my ass, and then dabbed the spot with a tissue.

"Just relax, Schnitzer," he said. "I'm taking you down to the city myself. The other paramedics are coming too. You'll be taken care of. Don't worry."

That spurred my long-term memory. The plan! Mengisto! I looked at my platoon again and saw his sorry ass standing there. I yelled out his name, I warned him not to go through with it, I told him what would happen if he tried. Except I didn't. The goddamned chemicals shut me up. And all of a sudden, I felt so tired. And the worries, all the chaos and the cold began to fade into warmth…a warmth that reminded me of my mother…of her cooking.

What happened next was this: I awoke in a hospital. I got treated with the utmost care. A few days passed and my company's mem pay journeyed down the mountain to pay me a visit. He asked how I was and I told him, "Fine". He gave me some book about the soldiers at Beaufort. I tried to read it, but it reminded me too much of Har Dov. I was jealous of the soldiers there; they'd given up the base eventually, blown it to hell and high water and left it for Lebanon. I wished we could do the same to Har Dov. I gave up reading the book three chapters in. The next day, they let me out of the hospital.

I got a week of sick leave so I went home. I thought about the base and I tried to call a few people. Nobody picked up. No reception on Har Dov. I worried about Mengisto. What if he went through with it and there was no paramedic around for a hundred clicks? What if he got hypothermia and nobody knew what to do? I drove myself half-crazy with what-ifs. How greatly I'd misjudged the plan's outcomes, the worst possible ones. Jail seemed downright cushy next to death.

So I prayed. And prayed. And prayed to an almighty I believed in but hated that Mengisto would never go guard at Guard Post Orange, and that if he really had to, that he'd leave the ice in the kitchen and off his nuts.

When the week passed and I found myself in uniform, sitting in an armored truck, only then did I remember how much I had to look forward to.

As we started that slow climb up the mountain, I saw the green around me get swathed in white. I heard the chirping of birds die away, leaving that familiar eerie quiet. Nothing lived up there but us. And just barely. I watched civilization fade into nothing and the antennas and metal fences rise on the horizon, clouded by fog. The base. That castle in its endless blizzard. I swear the sight made my very heart shrivel.

When the truck stopped and the door opened, the first thing my eyes met was Levi, waiting to greet me.

"Good, you're here!" he said.

He grabbed one of my bags and put his arm around my shoulder as if we were buddies.

"How are you feeling?" he asked.

"I'm fi—" I tried.

"Good. Listen. There aren't enough soldiers on base right now. So you got to go check your konenut, then head to Orange."

"Orange?" I asked, scared stiff. "Where is Meng—"

"No time to talk about it. I know this is fast, that you just got here. But there's no choice. We're all guarding more than we're breathing."

"Levi!" I said, "Where is Mengisto?"

"Go throw your bag in your room, then head up to the guard post. See you soon."

I'm not sure what it was I expected. Everybody I passed on my way to Orange was either too busy or too busy pretending to be busy to give me a second of their precious time. So cursing those *cocinelle-im*—meaning: transvestites—I headed straight for the guard post.

When I opened the door at Orange, an old nasty feeling and I became reacquainted. What I saw when I looked into that guard post set off the same reaction I'd known years ago, when I came back home from summer camp. Something had been off, very off, about my parents' apartment and it had freaked me out. I hadn't known how to describe it—this difference, which is when my mom had asked me, "How do you like the new wallpaper, honey?"

Orange was different too, but not because of the color of the walls or the piss-stench along its back. All was the same but the lookout—where two new plastic sheets now hung over the gaping space. They were windows. Then I noticed that plugged into the wall was a brand-spanking-new heater, warming up Orange so well, the place felt like a sauna. Next to it stood Fitness, sweating more than a cold drink.

I had barely begun to register what these renovations meant, when Fitness assaulted me. He would have called it a hug, I guess.

"Schnitzer!" he said. "You're back!"

"Hi, Fitness," I said, prying him off of me.

"How do you feel? Are you better?"

He aimed that big gay grin of his at me, looking so sincere it hurt.

"I'm fine, Fitness," I said, slipping past him to inspect the new windows. "I just...I just need a second."

He nodded. I could feel his eyes burrowing into my back.

"You know that you can go, right?" I told him. "Only one person's got to guard here."

"Not when there's fog," he said. "You know that!"

Sure enough, when I looked out those windows, fog looked back at me. I was stuck with the kid.

"What's wrong, Schnitzer?" he asked. "You know you can talk to me."

"Not now, Fitness."

"If it's about Mengisto..."

I whirled around to face him. "What do you know, Fitness?!" I asked. "Where is Mengisto?"

"You…you didn't hear?" he asked, stuttering. And just like that, Mr. Happy-Go-Lucky's smile faded. His eyebrows arched up, his lower lip quivered. Sensitive little shit was about to cry.

"No, no." I said. "Not now, Fitness, you little bachyan. You fucking tell me what happened."

"He…he's—"

"He's dead?!"

"No," Fitness said, looking confused. "Who told you that?"

"Kus'emek, Fitness! Just tell me already!"

Fitness nodded, more solemn than I'd ever seen him.

"He guarded here a few days ago…during the six-hour midnight shift. And you how know it gets so cold in this guard post? Well…how it used to?"

Fitness looked down at the miracle heater. I tried my best to be patient.

"So," Fitness continued, "I guess Mengisto forgot to bring his jacket or neck-warmer because he got really sick up here. He got so sick, he tried calling Maccabi for help. But you know…I don't know. Either the radio didn't work or nobody answered. Eventually he got so cold—I mean, so sick that at around three in the morning, he hit the war alarm."

He looked at the big red button on the wall beside him.

"When they heard it, everybody got up and ran out to their positions with full konenut on them…you know. It was our week to cover the guard posts so Berman came straight here. He's the one that found him. Berman says Mengisto was just lying there, collapsed on the floor."

Fitness looked me in the eye, looked down, made eye contact with me again then lowered it again.

"Because of what…what happened to you," Fitness said, "none of the paramedics were here. There were some guys with first-aid training who tried to help but…you know. The mem pay ordered the armored truck to come up and get Mengisto but it took forever because of the snow. They're saying he was already in deep by that point. Hypothermia."

Captive to the truth, it took all my will not to shriek.

"They brought him down to the hospital," Fitness said, "and last we heard, he slipped into a coma."

Fitness threw me a pitying look.

"You two are really good friends," he said, "and, you know, I understand. It's tough but it'll be okay."

Fitness started smiling again in an attempt, I guess, to comfort me. But that expression he wore, combined with the story he'd told awakened in me a rage so profound, I almost lost it.

"The weird thing is," Fitness went on, "that I was guarding that night too. At the same time. And, you know," Fitness shrugged, "it really wasn't that cold."

That did it. My hands flew up, wrapped around Fitness's neck and squeezed. His eyes bulged out like a cartoon's. He flailed his arms and legs at me with all his puny strength until he finally got a good knock to my side. The breath flew out of me and I loosened my grip.

"What are you…" he screamed, gasping, "Why—"

He didn't get another chance. I slammed my arms, legs, chest, everything I had against him into the wall with the windows. I wanted to make this jolly fucking cocinelle suffer. I wanted to break every bone in his body—no, I take that back. His mug was enough. I wanted to shatter his teeth, rip his jaw off—do anything to rearrange that dumb smile into a stuck ugly scowl. I let go of him again only to push him back even harder and heard a sound like plastic bending and cracking. Then a snap.

"Schnitzer!" he yelled. "The window—"

I grabbed his shirt in my fists and slammed him against the other wall. He suddenly cried out as his back arched. His back had hit something sticking out of the wall. But before I had a chance to see what it was, the sound gave me answer.

It really did make a miserable noise, that war alarm.

"Gentlemen," began the mem pay as he paced before us, "your platoon has been a part of this company for a total of two and half weeks and in this period of time, you have managed to sound the war alarm, a last resort saved for emergencies and I mean, real 'Hezbollah's invading!' emergencies, a total of four times. A new record, I believe. I congratulate you."

He stopped and looked at Udi.

"I'm sorry, did I say congratulate? I'm just going to assume you idiots don't understand sarcasm either and say this straight: You. Have. All. Fucked. Up. Big time."

"Why did he look at me when he said that?" Udi asked Berman under his breath. We sat in the mess hall—me, Fitness, Berman, Udi, Tooke, and the others whose names I've forgotten. Levi stood nearby, his back against a column with his arms crossed, shaking his head in disappointment, mouthing, *bizayon* at the floor over and over.

Bizayon, meaning: disgrace.

"I've considered asking each of you why you decided to treat this base like a fucking playground, but what's the point? None of you—not one of you has acted like a real lochem since you got here. Just a bunch of tzairim stuck in Basic Training. That's what I see."

Berman sat next to me. He yawned and rubbed his eyes, as if the mem pay were crooning a lullaby. Likely 'cause he didn't understand half the Hebrew the guy was spouting. Next to him sat Udi, eyes wide, panting even louder than usual. And there at the end of the bench sat Fitness, sporting a few fresh bruises but otherwise looking fine. Still upbeat somehow.

"This is how it works," the mem pay continued. "From now on, the alarms are all disabled. If by some chance, you do happen to see a bearded figure running at you, bombs strapped to his chest, screaming *allahu akbar*, you may call Maccabi and tell them so. Then, after Maccabi has verified it with Field Intel's cameras and been given permission, he will sound the alarm. Then and only then may you shoot the damned raghead. That clear?"

"Clear," we all said in unison. Or would have, if Tooke had just kept his dumb mouth shut.

"Sir!" Tooke said.

"Yes, Tooke?" the mem pay said, nearly groaning.

"Don't you think, sir, that going through all these bureaucratic entanglements in order to terminate a threat is dangerous, sir? Don't you think it'll take too long?"

"No," the mem pay said. "I don't, Tooke."

"But Sir—"

"Tooke, the likelihood that you will ever see—let alone kill— a terrorist in the entirety of your time here on Har Dov is next to none. This border's quieter than a dead baby."

"But sir—"

"And furthermore, if something were to happen, however unlikely, I'm confident that you would have more than enough time to get Maccabi's permission. Your life would never be at risk. Is that clear?"

"But—"

"I said, is that clear, Tooke?"

Tooke did not try again. He just nodded, subdued. Then the mem pay turned and strode out of the mess hall. We all sat there, quiet for a minute or two. I chanced a look at Fitness again and saw him stare back at me. I turned away.

"Bizayon," Levi muttered. He might as well have branded it to us in scarlet.

Later that day, I talked to Berman and asked him what had really happened to Mengisto. Same story, it turned out. Then Levi sat me down and gave me a lecture on violence and fighting and bizayon this and bizayon that, which I found very informative and inspirational, of course. Udi and Berman argued over Disney movies, whether they sounded better in Hebrew or English, and I listened, pretending to be entertained.

I avoided Fitness the best I could, but he caught me eventually. He told me he wanted to apologize. He didn't know what for, but he was sorry anyways. He smiled the most honest fucking smile I'd ever seen and said, "I know you guys think that I'm always happy but I'm not. I just try to act that way so you guys will too."

I shouldn't have accepted his apology. I should have said, "You did nothing wrong. I'm the one that's sorry." But I didn't. I just took what he had to give and walked away. Only now, all these years later, do I really regret that. Kid may have been obnoxious, but he was the only real man there. Because while everyone else just pretended to follow the Warrior Code, only Fitness laughed back at his suffering, challenged it to conquer his natural optimism. I never would have thought I'd say this, but Fitness; he was the only real lochem our platoon had.

Guard duty resumed that day. A few techies came to disable the big red war buttons and we watched them, feeling impotent. The fog died down around four in the afternoon, so I left Fitness to guard Orange by himself. I told him I'd be back in an hour to switch with him.

Just as I was pulling my vest off in the hangar, looking forward to a good forty winks, somebody pushed me from behind. I face-planted into the cement, rolled around and took a look at my assailant. Surprise, surprise.

"You think I forgot you?" the Beard asked.

I nearly rolled my eyes.

"Really?" I asked. "You really got nothing better to do?"

He walked over, kneeled down, and grabbed a fistful of my uniform.

"I should fuck you up, tzair," he said.

"Yeah. And everybody from my platoon along with me?"

"Don't fuck around. I know you hit the alarm twice by yourself."

"No," I said, shaking my head. "You don't get it. If you're going to fuck me up, you'll have to deal with them too."

I glanced over his shoulder at the shipping container barracks and nodded my head toward them. He turned to look for himself at my cavalry, or lack thereof, and that's when I jabbed the son of a bitch right in his ugly bearded kisser.

The fight didn't last long. Just as the guys ran over to pull us off of each other, the Beard managed to slam his gun's stock into my forehead. I wish I'd passed out. Instead I was left with a flash then a throbbing pain, the sound of Levi screaming, "Again?!" and the Beard's laughter as he walked away, victorious.

"Kid's got balls," he said to one of his friends, "but he's just a kid. Tzair."

"You," Levi said to the Beard. "Get out of here. You're supposed to be in the Comm. Branch."

"Relax, Levi," he said. "Only one's person got to be in there at a time. I made sure somebody would cover me, while I dealt with him."

He pointed at me, smirking.

"I don't give a shit," Levi said. "Get back there now."

"Yes, mefaked!"

The Beard mock-saluted him and ran off with his posse, laughing all the while.

"What were you thinking?" Levi asked me.

Without another word, I got up and walked to my room. I needed sleep. I needed just a little bit of shut-eye. Alone. Away from Udi and Berman and Tooke and Levi and the Beard and Fitness and Mengisto. Especially Mengisto. From all that I'd done to him.

I turned off the lights, collapsed onto my cot, and prayed that sleep would find me, that I could somehow flush away the pain and the anger for a few minutes. My head ached from that butt to the head. I lay there, trying to ignore the feeling, to let loose my mind, to let it wander into dreams. Who knows how long I waited there in the dark. At some point, my surroundings caved into nothing, a quiet blanket enveloped me and that's when the door flew open.

"Get up, Schnitzer," Levi said. "You're guarding in ten minutes."

I swore. I got out of bed; I listened once again to Levi recite the rules for guard duty and I started to walk toward the konenut locker. That's when I heard it.

A shrill whistle, its pitch descending. Lower, then lower, then lower until it was no more than a whispered whoosh. A distant explosion. A battering of metal, concrete collapsing into an erupting furnace. A sick, low moan, maybe an aftershock. Not lightning or thunder this time, baby. A bona fide fucking rocket.

A second later the siren wailed. Without hesitation, we all ran to the locker, threw on our konenut, strapped on our helmets, and dashed out the hangar only to stop outside, awe-stricken. There along the ridge of the base's catwalk billowed out a mammoth pillar of smoke. It came from a guard post. Levi screamed at me but I didn't hear him. One thing and one thing only made sense to me at that moment: the guard post was Orange. Fitness was in there.

120

We sprinted up there as fast as our feet could take us, grabbing hoses and fire extinguishers along the way. About a hundred meters away, we could go no further. That reeking smoke shrouded the whole catwalk so thick we could barely breathe. Berman ran down to the hangar to get gas masks and by the time he got back the smoke had spread further. We strapped the gas masks on, checked that they were working, and then ran into the hot black cloud.

We killed the fire quick, spraying white and water everywhere. It hadn't caught on to much, other than the plastic and electronics. What was left of Orange was nothing but burning rubble and spark-spitting cables and blood and body parts. I wanted to pull him out, to save whatever was left of him, but they held me back. I screamed through the gas mask. I wailed. I burst into tears and ripped off the mask, only to start coughing in a mad fit. They pried me away from the guard post's ruins, pulled me away from Fitness 'until I was out of the smoke and gasping for air. I tried to run back and they held me. I hit everything in sight in my senseless tantrum. And that was before I knew what had really happened.

How Fitness had spotted three suspicious figures climbing up a hill on the Lebanese side maybe four clicks away. How he had reported to Maccabi the unusual then suspicious then downright threatening activity and how the Beard, since it was his shift at the Comm. Branch, had told Fitness to shut it. How he'd told him to stop making shit up. And how those three figures had fired a mortar rocket into Orange, blowing the whole guard post to smithereens and Fitness along with it.

I learned the truth later, on a patrol along the suddenly action-packed Lebanese border, jutting in and out of Israel proper, hunting down terrorists. Tooke told me the whole story.

"You must be joking."

"I'm not."

"You aren't joking?"

"No."

"What are you, crazy?! This army can't compete with America's!"

Udi and Berman were at it again. Tooke, thankfully, was out of ear-shot, busy manning the machine gun up top. Our new mefaked sat near the driver in the front. As for me, I'd gotten the best seat in the house, squashed between cardboard boxes full of cardboard food and the blaring radio. The big metal machine driving us, a *nakpadon*—meaning: soldier carrier, looked a bit like a tank without its turret, a sort of tailless dog or castrated man. And it huffed and puffed out so much smoke, we learned how to breathe the shit like air.

We drove constantly. Some days we remained within ha'aretz. Some days we ventured out. From inside the nakpadon, I couldn't really tell the difference.

Progress, the mem pay told us, took time. But this—this was a fuck-ing tortoise race. The whole company traveled via nakpadon through the contested Shebba Farms, along the Blue Line. Our target: to hunt down Hezbollah. Our success: little.

Truth is, our sole responsibility was cleaning up after the air force's messes; whatever didn't get bombed to hell was left for us to pillage. The pilots got the heavy lifting, those soaring cowards, barraging the enemy with a joystick from a hundred clicks away. Kids and their video games.

After Fitness's death, it took another three terrorist attacks along the border and a soldier's kidnapping to make the army budge. Only then had they given us the order to climb down Har Dov and begin mobilizing for a small operation.

I still thought about Fitness often. I reckon we all did. After all the rubble and equipment and carnage at Orange had been cleared out, two things still remained missing: Fitness's legs. We never found them. They rebuilt the guard post and our men continued to guard there, as if nothing had ever happened. But to this day I hear that soldiers on their six-hour shifts tell stories about the haunted legs, and how at night you can sometimes hear them ambling about.

The radio suddenly blared, making me jump.

"Gimel Two, Gimel Two from Anglia," it said.

I grabbed the handset, climbed over Udi and Berman, and handed it to the new mefaked. He took it and switched the loudspeaker off.

As he spoke, I heard Udi mention Levi.

"That malamnik!" he said. "How many asses you think he had to kiss to get into officer's school?"

"I can't believe Doron Levi will be a mem mem," Berman said. "What an *oketz*!"

Oketz, meaning: sting, but in this case: a soldier who cheats their way out of work.

"Received," the new mefaked said. "Schnitzer, grab the handset."

I clambered past Udi and Berman again, grabbed the handset and returned it to the radio.

"Tooke, come down here for a second," said the new mefaked, pulling on his pant leg. "I got news for you guys. We've just arrived at the bottom of Beaufort. You've heard of it, right? The mountain we used to occupy?"

We all nodded. I remembered the book the mem pay had given me.

"We're starting our ascent right now," he said. "Be ready—we may meet resistance up top at the fortress. That clear?"

We nodded again. I glanced at Udi and Berman. Just a second ago, they'd been laughing, fucking around. Now they looked so serious. What did that to us—took away our laughter, made us so damn numb? Hell, Udi barely even bitched anymore. There wasn't a bachyan amongst us. How arbitrary seemed the Warrior Code now that we were at war. Real war. Maybe lochemim didn't laugh or cry. Maybe they felt nothing.

"One more thing," the mefaked said. "Your friend from your platoon, the one that's been in a coma—I don't know how to pronounce his name. They told me to tell you that he woke up. He's fine."

The new mefaked turned back toward the driver. I looked at Berman and Udi and Tooke. I did not know what to say. I had become so used to bad news and how to take it. But this? How the hell was I supposed to react to this?

"Wait," Tooke said to the mefaked. "You're saying Mengisto is fine?"

"Yeah, that's his name," the mefaked said.

"So when's he coming back to the platoon?" Udi asked.

"No," the mefaked said, shaking his head. "There's no way he'll stay a lochem. He'll either get a job or a shortened service."

My god. It had worked after all. I had only just said how dead, how numb I felt, and yet now I sensed something bubbling up inside me— some shade of a feeling I used to know and the strangeness of it all tore into me and made me want to cry out a *baruch hashem* or *hallelujah* or *allahu akbar*. Praise some lord of some kind.

Udi said, "Wow."

I said, "Mengisto..."

Berman said, "Yeah. What an oketz."

I looked at Berman. Tooke and Udi looked at Berman and then we all burst out into the most painful laughter. We laughed so hard, our throats ripped raw, our sides ached, our eyes burned with held back tears. We laughed until we couldn't and then we laughed some more, clutching onto each other's shoulders desperately. We might have collapsed into a heap on the nakpedon's floor were it not for that sweaty embrace.

The new mefaked gawked at us, puzzled. The driver beside him pressed his foot against the pedal, pushed the tank up the mountain toward this other castle in its endless blizzard, and we lochemim laughed and laughed the whole way there, defying the menace that loomed before us with our fleeting joy.

124

OPERATION GET SOME: PART II

Aaron Klotsky was pissed. He'd been stood up before, sure. But never by another guy.

Leaving the rendezvous point behind, he stomped along the alleyways of Nahlaot toward his little spartan apartment in a huff. Aaron assumed that there must have been a good reason for Yoav to bail. He further assumed that it must have involved debauchery of colossal proportions—perhaps a ménage à trois or a new membership in the mile high club or some public display of aphrodisia--in which case he would fully respect and furthermore encourage the absence of his dear friend. But this, Aaron's gut had to admit, seemed unlikely.

The fact was, Aaron knew the whims and quirks of his Israeli friend far too well and could therefore guess with relative accuracy Yoav's excuse for having stood him up. It went like this: Yoav being Yoav was only in the early stages of getting some. Not because he lacked finesse, per se, but rather due to the relish he took in toying with his prey. Yoav adored the prolonged chase, the preceding moments before the act itself, and this led Aaron to believe that his friend still had a ways to go.

Maybe it's better that way, Aaron thought. *I don't have to tell him yet.*

He knew what he sounded like and cursed his own cowardice. But to tell your best friend, the one that considers you a hero and mentor, that everything you've taught him is bullshit, took the kind of balls Aaron didn't have. Yoav would argue the opposite, but then—picking up girls had never been Aaron's weakness. Honesty, on the other hand…

It was at this juncture in his worried ruminations, that Aaron Klotsky reached the front door of his apartment.

"Hey!" he yelled out, opening the door. "You home?"

"I'm out here!" a muffled falsetto voice answered.

He moved through the hallways, noticing a poster of Audrey Hepburn on the living room wall and a vase filled with carnations on the kitchen counter and the chemical scent of cleaning products everywhere. In the midget living room he looked toward the glass doors at its end. There, leaning on the rails of the balcony, overlooking Sacher Park, stood the girl.

He opened the doors and she turned to meet him.

"I like what you've done with the place," he said.

"Liar," she said, smiling. "Too girly for you, isn't it?"

Laughing, he told her, "You could paint the walls pink for all I care. I'm just glad I got somebody to share it with."

She grinned and shook her head.

"You're a hopeless romantic, Aaron Klotsky."

He nodded, leaned in.

"Who would have thought?"

They called her Anabelle.

It'd been a long time since Yoav had been presented with such a formidable challenge of the female form, which, of course, only further intensified his excitement. No, the word "excitement" does not quite do Yoav's feelings justice. So swagger-less and humble had their first few minutes together left him, so fully enthralled by Anabelle and her apparent indifference to all his efforts, Yoav had not noticed a thing outside Operation Get Some. This included the missed phone calls and texts from his friend Aaron Klotsky.

After a short walk and further verbal foreplay, he and she had parted, Yoav numberless but with a planned date that very evening. Now he sprinted to his apartment as fast as his feet could take him.

Yoav put Luck away the first chance he got. Her role had been to draw the prey, and however admirably she had performed, a bar was no place for an M-16.

He hung the uniform, showered, changed into jeans and a black button-up, rolled up the sleeves, put on his kicks, and barged out the door as quick as he'd come.

Much remained to do before evening's end.

"We're not gonna fuck. You get that, right?"

All the planning in the world, all the back-up steps, the cheap compliments, the lengths taken to listen and purchased drinks, could not have prepared Yoav for this. He had known from the moment he first saw Anabelle that she was not your typical girl. But this—this evening and the conversations that pervaded it—had wholly floored Yoav.

Never had he met an American girl so damn prickly. So damn Israeli, if you will.

"Eh—" he started. "What? Sorry?"

"I said," she said, "that you and I, we're not gonna fuck."

"It was the last thing on my mind," Yoav tried.

She snorted.

"You expect me to believe that?"

"It's the truth!"

"Yoav," she said, laying her hand on his arm. "It's okay. You can drop the act. Why ask me out, take me to Sideways, keep the drinks coming, and try so hard to be charming without any agenda? You want to get laid."

Yoav looked at her, the color in his eyes a dark orange now, trying to pry her green pair open. He wanted—no, he needed to crack the anomaly that was Annabelle. A few seconds passed. He decided to play it straight... for a while anyway

"Fine," he said. "You win. I wanted to get some tonight."

"There we go," she said, grinning. "Now, doesn't it feel better getting that off your chest?"

"But here's what I don't understand: why did you say yes to me today at the *shuk*? Why even show up here tonight?"

She paused. Her eyes wandered away toward the bar. Again he noticed that neck.

"I don't know. I guess because you interest me. I mean, you've got the most see-through game ever, but there's still...something."

Yoav let out a "tsk" and shook his head.

"Bullshit," he said.

"What? Why do you say that?"

"I don't buy it," he said, smiling. "I think you came here for the same reasons I did."

"Not all American girls are sluts, you know," she said, a sudden fury in her tone. This delighted Yoav. Now he knew it would work.

"But they sure are easy compared to Israeli girls."

"Oh really?" she asked, not asking.

"Yes, really," he answered, grinning.

"Why do all guys think that?"

"Because it's true—American girls put out. Israeli girls don't."

"Oh, come on. I know plenty of square American girls and whoreish Israelis. That's a generalization."

"It sure is. And an accurate one. You want to know the truth, Annabelle?"

She waited.

"*Nu?*" he asked, "Well do you?"

"Get on with it."

"It's like this," Yoav began. "Israeli girls—at least, the city kind—are by and large a bunch of snobs. They're born and raised princesses, self-obsessed bitches who go to clubs just to tease us poor Israeli schnooks. They have no daddy issues, they have no concerns of self-worth and they feel no need for casual sex."

"And American girls are the opposite, right?" Anabelle asks.

"That's right. American girls put out because they're fucking needy and desperate for love. They over and over again mistake a guy's interest for sex as something more than that. They're gullible and they're sad and they crave comfort."

He stopped and looked at her.

"And that includes you too."

"Fuck you."

She took out her purse and looked in it for something.

"You wanted the truth," Yoav said. "You got it."

"Have any gum?" she asked.

Yoav pulled out a stick of gum from his left pocket and handed it to her.

"Sorry if it upsets you but it's just—"

"There's one thing you're not taking into account," she said, pulling the paper wrapper off the gum.

"What's that?" he asked, genuinely curious.

"What about the girls who are just as horny as the guys?"

Yoav hesitated.

"Watch out, Anabelle," he said. "You're in danger of becoming a walking cliché."

She dropped the gum into her mouth and chewed.

"You want to keep psychoanalyzing me here?"

She stopped chewing. "Or do you want to do it elsewhere?"

Yoav turned to the bartender. "Check please."

Luck lay next to the bed. She watched as Yoav and Anabelle burst into the apartment, a single gyrating body. She watched them strip bare, each the other, watched them collapse onto the bed, tumble through sheets, clumsy legs swinging. She watched her pull his jagged fingers into her, watched her arch that never-ending neck, watched her auburn hair splinter across the white pillow.

Luck's jealousy knew no boundaries.

Yoav breathed heavy as a basset hound. Anabelle didn't moan so much as hiccup. He wanted to quit the foreplay quick; the night's parley had been, for him, plenty stimulating. She, on the other hand, had different plans. Yoav started to fumble about and she stopped him. She pushed his shoulders down, beckoning him to get acquainted with her lower half.

He complied.

She tasted like pineapple juice, which he appreciated. She writhed like an epileptic and one of her thighs crashed into his left temple, making him dizzy.

"Sorry," she gasped.

"It's alright," he managed, getting back to work.

In all the years he'd flattered, smooth-talked, and bullshitted, never had Yoav's tongue been so tired. Each time he tried to climb back up, kissing his way up her chest, she would just gently nudge his head back down.

As long as she'd repay the favor, Yoav bore no grievances. Ten more minutes passed and Anabelle started to seize up, quivering. Then shaking. Yoav dived in as mad as he could muster. *Just get it over with*, he thought. *Then it'll be her turn.*

He anticipated this moment with such uninhibited glee, that when she finally came and he jerked his head back to watch her collapse onto the compromised bed, panting and sweating, he laughed.

"Alright, Anabelle," he said, climbing up to her. "What do you say?"

She looked at him, her eyes half-closed, and smiled.

"Thank you," she said.

Then she took the sheets, wrapped them around herself and turned on her side, closing her eyes. Yoav stared at her, confounded.

"Wha—" he started. "What?"

Anabelle did not answer and very soon her breathing grew softer and less rapid and she seemed at peace. Yoav couldn't believe it; he'd been swindled. That afternoon at the shuk, she must have seen him as just an opportunity to get some., With subtlety and wit, she had used his obvious infatuation with her to manipulate him into thinking Operation Get Some was his own.

Yoav had to admit it. He admired the bitch.

When he awoke the next morning, Yoav could not move. Aaron Klotsky and other Americans would diagnose this particular affliction as "blue balls". Anabelle was awake, putting clothes back on. He watched her for a moment, regaining both his consciousness and utter humiliation. He glanced at the bedside table, at her purse and its spilled contents, and noticed something odd.

There, lying next to a cell phone, some keys, an empty gum wrapper, and a small makeup bag was an army-issued wallet. An Israeli army-issued wallet, one identical to his own. He reached for it, opened the wallet, and stared in disbelief into the face of a smiling Anabelle surrounded by Hebrew. Anabelle's Army ID.

"You!" he said. "You're a soldier?!"

"Good morning to you too," she said, turning her bare back toward him, smiling.

"Wait—" he stuttered, "Please explain."

She pulled the straps of her bra over her shoulders and then reached behind her back to clip it.

"Did I not mention it?" she asked, "I'm a Lone Soldier."

"You're a Lone Soldier?! Like Aaron?"

"Who's Aaron?"

Yoav sat up in the bed, shaking his head.

"I can't believe this," he said.

"What's wrong?" she asked, and now she turned around to face him. "Did I confuse you because I wasn't in uniform? I'm guarding for a Birthright group this week. I was at the shuk with the American kids."

It all clicked. Yoav looked at Annabelle, laughed, and then collapsed back onto the bed. But this hurt and he cringed. His balls still killed him. He let out a low moan and closed his eyes. He heard her shuffling about. He heard her open a phone and click into the keypad; he assumed she was texting. He heard her snap the phone shut and then felt her get closer to him. She whispered into his ear.

"I have to go now. But I actually had a good time. See you around, Yoav."

She kissed his cheek and then she left.

Yoav looked over at Luck.

"Don't you judge me," he told her. "I'm not used to being used."

Yoav told the tale in its entirety to Aaron Klotsky the next day at Aaron's apartment. Aaron snorted and guffawed every couple of seconds, stopped Yoav at multiple points to throw in his own anecdotes, as was customary, and patted Yoav on the back over and over, saying in his horrible accent, "*Misken*! *Misken*!"

Or: "Poor guy! Poor guy!"

When Yoav reached the climax, literal and figurative, Aaron fell onto the floor, got up, ran around the apartment in circles, howled, slapped every knee in sight, and then concluded his fit by hugging Yoav. Hard.

"I'm sorry, buddy," Aaron said, still laughing.

"That's alright," Yoav told him. "I guess it makes a good story."

They both calmed down and grew quiet. Aaron's amused grin faded.

"I've got something to tell you too, man," Aaron said.

"What is it?"

"I've got a girlfriend. There! I said it! Done! What do you want to do tonight? Want to hit up Mike's Place?"

"Wait—what?" Yoav said. "Did you just say you have a girlfriend?"

"Yeah," Aaron said.

Yoav frowned.

"That's weird. I mean, congratulations and all. But that's weird. You're the one who always said—"

"Girlfriends are for suckers. Yeah, I know."

Yoav looked at Aaron and wanted to be happy for him but no luck.

"I thought this place looked funny," Yoav said. "The decorations, I mean."

"Listen—" Aaron started. "This doesn't change shit. We're still gonna go out and meet girls. I'm your wingman."

"Yeah, alright. I gotta go, man. I'll call you later."

Yoav got up and headed for the door. He stopped.

"One question: is she Israeli or American?"

Aaron smiled. "Israeli."

"One more question," Yoav said. "How'd she snag you?"

Aaron shrugged. "She was the first girl to ever tell me, 'No.'"

Yoav nodded, waved with two fingers and left his ex-mentor Aaron Klotsky behind. Wingmen, Yoav understood, they would never be again.

Later that day, Yoav opened his cell phone. He began to scroll through the contact list and stopped. There was a new phone number listed there that he did not recognize—somebody addressed as "A." with a smiley face next to the name. It took him a second to figure it out. Then he shook his head and snapped the phone shut.

It looked like Luck had a real competitor.

THE TOURIST

The grains of sand, they dance.
    They swerve and gambol
    among the asphalt shambles of a passage
    as the wheels advance.
    At their intrepid deliberate rate,
    they pendulate along the sand without presage.

The driver of the Hummer receives a text message
    and checks his phone.
The mem mem beside him dozes,
    exposes his gaping mouth
    to his scheming soldiers' funny bone.
Udi reaches across the seat
and, in between the sleeping man's split lips,
he slips a piece of onion-flavored Bissli.
    He retreats.

The mem mem lurches forward.
He coughs, he gasps. He asks,
    "Who did that?!"
His eyes dart toward the back seat,
at Gal and Udi, mouths muzzled,
though the eyes unearth their furtive mirth.
No more puzzled by the salty snack's source,

the mem mem castes forth his sweaty palm and says,
     "You little shits. Gimme some more."

Just as Udi begins to pour the Bissli
into Mem Mem Levi's outstretched hand
the radio roars with activity.
     "Nesher from 72, do you copy?"
Grabbing the handset, the mem mem blows twice into the mic.
     "I read you, 72."
"Root," replies the radio. "You've got a Tourist two clicks north of your
position."
     The mem mem's posture stiffens.
     Udi and Gal and the driver listen.
"Sorry, 72," the mem mem mumbles. "Repeat that, please."
"A tourist," says the voice. "Two clicks north. Now, hurry."

The driver glances at the mem mem, who nods his head
and whispers, "*Nu?*"
     The driver's foot descends.
On cue, the engine roars its stern devotion.
Motion and the Hummer blur.
The tires sever the sand-dune floor,
aim away from the gilded ocean
to the edge of the asphalt shore.

Over the Hummer's hum,
the mem mem hollers into the mic,
the driver slips the mobile against his thigh
and Udi chews the knuckle on his right thumb.
As for Gal, he eyes with fresh interest

the instrument he's held by his side since his enlistment:
    the gun.

It is a totem to all Gal has not done.
The only bullets bled from its barrel
remain buried in barren hills and cardboard.
Gal, the so-called warrior, believes himself
no more than a plastic green figurine, his M-4, a BB gun.
    Games for bloodthirsty boys.
The kind called "just for fun."

But...
Gal knows what a tourist means.
The truth gleams in the refracted rays of the sun,
promising to quench a thirst,
to fulfill the perverse purpose
of a soldier and a soldier's gun.

One
kilometer away from the rushing hummer,
spotted by 72's spy balloon,
    stands the stranger.
He crossed the border,
    sprinted to the fence and clambered over.
Had he passed another line
in another country,
he would likely have been classified:
    illegal immigrant.
But by the divide of Israel and Gaza,
    no crosser is innocent.

The mem mem straps the helmet to his crown,
readjusts its mushroom-cloud netting,
turns toward his soldiers,
says,
  "You ready?"
Gal and Udi nod giddy guts-hungry shakes.
"Like in the exercises," the mem mem reminds them.
"No shock. No mistakes."

The Hummer skids to a halt.
  Burnt asphalt fills their nostrils as they unsnap their seatbelts.
"Let's go!" the mem mem bellows.
Gal kicks open his door, pulls the M-4 to his chest,
falls to one knee and aims each eye at the tourist.

He stands fifty meters from the fence.
He wears knock-off Adidas kicks
  and ripped jeans.
His face is bruised, his lip split.
His eyes brim blue.
He cannot be older than fifteen.

"Get down!" the mem mem screams.
  He tries again in mangled Arabic.
The boy does not shift, nor move a muscle;
a derelict he indeed does seem
but his eyes are wide. Terrified.
  Only then does Gal notice the black bag by the boy›s side.

"Levi," Gal whispers, "Look! Next to his foot."

It takes the mem mem a moment to register the sight.
He cocks his weapon.
"You too," he tells Udi and Gal.
Gal follows suit and feels,
    as the bullet slithers into the chamber,
the sweat of thrill and the throb of dread.
    Danger he so long coveted.

The mem mem squints at Gal and says,
"Keep your thumb on the safety,
and your index on the trigger,
If he moves, you do not hesitate."
Gal nods.
    Half a second is all it takes
to slide from safe to semi,
and squeeze a finger.
    The odds Gal will kill today just grew greater.

As the mem mem scrambles into the Hummer,
to amplify the radio,
Gal and Udi fix their eyes and barrels
upon the Gazan boy.
    "He's young," Udi says.
"Don't let him fool you," Gal replies.
"I'm just saying—I expected…"
    "What? A kalash and keffiyeh? Don›t be an idiot."
"It's just…I don't know. A surprise."

The tourist stands very still,
    as if petrified.

His blue eyes water
and, despite himself, Gal wonders "Why?"

Why does he cry and from what does he run?
    The swollen misshaped face,
    the bruises, the blood.
What phantom did this tourist chase,
    to so mutilate his form?

    Or could this countenance be contrived?
Might the boy's bedraggled state
hide a plot more malevolent,
hide the carefully disguised element of
        hate?
The tourist waits and he pouts
to solicit their sympathies, no doubt—
waits until the time is right
        to pounce.

Gal tells himself he's ready.

"Udi!"
the mem mem yells.
    Udi shuffles into the Hummer quickly,
leaving Gal alone with the boy.

They watch one another.
The Tourist shifts his gaze toward the Hummer,
then back to Gal.
    His first unfurls.

Between the iron joints of the M-4,
Gal's fingers fidget.
      The index curls.

The tourist points to the bag at his feet
and nods toward Gal.
Gal shakes his head,
as if to say,
      "You move, you're dead."
The tourist waits,
      then begins to descend.

Eyes fixed upon the M-4,
the boy lowers his arm toward the bag.
      "Don't do that!" Gal whispers.
His whole life, his heart never beat quicker.
He watches as the Arab boy's hand
slowly moseys toward the bag's zipper
      and again he whimpers, "Don't do that!"

The tourist touches the metal
      and proceeds to unzip.
Gal just stares, staggered and stripped of his mettle.
The trigger, he tries and fails to grip.

He sees
      the hand submerged into the innards of the bag,
      the eyes of the tourist burrow into his.
He hears the screams, the scuffles from the Hummer,
sees the dark blotch rise in the withdrawn fist.

Gal's eyes focus.
The tourist stands
with a sweatshirt in his hand.

"Gal!"
Gal hears the mem mem
sprawl onto the sand beside him.
"Gal," he says, "what happened to you? Are you alright?"
"I'm…" he stutters. "I'm fine."

Gal and the mem mem stand.
They cover Udi as he accosts the tourist
    who presents his sweatshirt
and gestures toward the rest of his possessions:
    sandals, clothes, a magazine.

They tie the boy's hands behind his back.
They blindfold him.
They do not speak.
    Within two minutes, three Sufa jeeps swarm the scene.
They transport him back to base
and, on orders,
the soldiers and mem mem guard their captured tourist
    and wait.

The mem mem asks the boy his name.
    "Khalid," he says.
The mem mem asks him why he came.
Khalid hesitates.
    "I heard here…here was a better place."

Together the soldiers gape at the boy,
    this sorry eyeful.
Then the driver unflips his cell phone and ambles away.
Udi stays,
while the mem mem unties the blindfold
and looks Khalid eye to eye.
    As for Gal,
he peers into his hands as if to redraw the lines.

He thanks and hates whatever angel held his finger.
    Within him
the anger and joy run rampant together.
Today he could have killed his friends
    and yet,
this dread to pull the trigger,
which he damns,
    let live an innocent man.

A boy.
He looks at the bruises on Khalid,
    sees how he misconstrued them.
He looks at the bloody lip and sees how it split.
    Who abused him?

"Who did this to you?" Gal asks the boy in Hebrew.
Khalid turns questioningly to the mem mem.
He translates.
    The boy inhibits himself at first, looking both ways.
He double-takes as if his aggressor might emerge from the walls.
The terror creeps into the corners of his face.

It crawls
from the tremors in his fingers
to the rapid pulse of his heart-rate.
        The blue eyes of Khalid meet the brown of Gals'.
He answers, "My father."

The words are neither true nor false.
        For what father could be called a father
when this razed flesh is his son?
        Khalid is that rare breed of boy—
Brave
        to run.

Gal looks away,
looks at the metal in his splayed hands.
He had always craved to fire this gun,
        until the crucial moment came.
He will never forget the shame
but he will forgive it.
For every minute Khalid lives is, to Gal,
        sacred.

Gal looks at Levi.
At Udi. At Khalid.
He hears Udi say, "So guys, what do you think?"
The mem mem asks, "What?"
"Do you think he likes Bissli?"

CHARLATAN

From the leaf blossoms a green berry. It fattens and bulges and the color of its cratered skin turns white, yellow then rust. So born is the orange and all the other oranges that dangle beside it. In half a second, they all bloom into full ripe being, spitting juice from their stems, swaying back and forth from their sudden birth. This as the girl sprints past the orange tree. And every tree after.

She runs through the grove and waves of orange gush alongside her. As she passes, the empty trees burst full with color and heft and that acidic scent. Her bare feet skim the floor of leaves and twigs. What she hears drowning out the drum of her own heartbeat is a moan and splintering sound as the branches sink down with their new weight.

The girl stops and looks over her shoulder. She looks for him, seeming scared but somehow eager. Before her figure the branches are vacant. Behind her—where she watches—they are full. Then she sees them change; the faraway branches rise. Their oranges fall to the floor, decay into black peels and rancid juice. The trees of the grove let leave their color. As he runs toward her, his feet sink into a carpet of rotted fruit.

She turns and tears away, darting in and out of the aisles of the grove. The oranges burst into life wherever she moves. And as he follows her, they drop dead.

She peeks over her shoulder as she runs, taunting him with her trembling grin. She knows him but he terrifies her still.

She chances another glance and sees nothing. No sign of him. She slows to a standstill and tries to quiet her breathing. Brushing aside the

145

few bangs from her forehead, she waits. Then she hears the sound of his footsteps. From her left—no, from her right they come.

Oranges fall from either side. She turns forward to run again and stops. There he stands before her, his eyes hungry. He snatches her forearm, coarse fingers snaking their way around her flesh. She pants. She sweats. He puts his palm to her forehead, feels the fever in her. The trees on either side of the girl and the man are lop-sided, half dead. Still clutching onto her wrist, he steps toward her.

"Why do you always run?" he asks.

"More fun this way," she says. "Don't you think?"

Her smile is defiant. He leans in his lips to the sweat of her brow, about to kiss her there, like a father might his child. But she grabs his neck with her free arm and pulls his mouth to hers. In between entangled tongues and the shared hot breath, she whispers, "I'm not a little girl."

They fall onto the floor, onto the bed of rotting oranges and strip each other bare. His fingertips graze her slight curves. Her back and hair wet, covered in juice. She shivers.

"You're wrong," he says, stopping. "This is—"

Then she grabs his fingers and pulls him into her.

"Not as long as you're dreaming."

Jeremy's eyes open. The girl and the orange grove are gone, a metal slate in their place. He stares at it, the upper bunk of his cot, and exhales. He'd been holding his breath. Rowdy snores and the shuffling of sleeping bags. He turns his head to glance at the other soldiers asleep in the barracks. They too dream, relish these few precious hours to be away from base.

Jeremy looks down at his watch, reads the date and then lays his head back down on the pillow. His eyes close. He imagines it all. He pictures the endless grove, the floor of orange peels, the juice in her hair and sweat on her skin. He begs the same dream to revisit him. But it refuses. He lies there for minutes, maybe more, daring it to. But the dream is gone. At last, fatigue sways him and just as all the activity in Jeremy's mind hushes, his nostrils twitch. They catch an odd scent. Something like citrus.

Jeremy's hand knocks on the door. His dress uniform looks no better than a rag, drenched in sweat and dust. He tries his best to assemble himself. He tucks in his shirt and straightens the red beret on his shoulder. The door opens and a nervous woman doused in makeup pulls him forward and kisses him on either cheek.

"Jeremy!" she says. "Why do you always knock? Come in, come in."

"Hi, Ronit." he says.

Air-conditioning hits him at full blast along with the scent of baharat and onions.

"Smells good." he says.

"It should," she says. "Tonight is a very important night."

"It is?"

Ronit hesitates then says, "Go say hello to the girls."

"Sure, where are they?"

"Yarden just got home a couple minutes ago. I think she's in her room. Go say hi."

She bustles off toward the kitchen without another word. A bit bewildered, Jeremy turns around. He goes through the hallway to the door at its end.

"Yarden?" he yells out. "Got clothes on?"

"Jeremy!" a voice calls out from behind the door. Then it flies open, a hand thrusts forward, pulls him into the room, and slams the door.

"Thank god you're here!" she says, hugging him quick and bolting to her closet. "You won't believe what I've been through."

He raises his eyebrows and grins.

"Nothing changes around here, does it?" he says.

"My mother has invited Roger—remember him? He's her new boyfriend. I told you about him. She invited him to Shabbat dinner."

"Really? Is this that same guy—"

"Yeah. The American one. Guess there'll be a lot of English speaking tonight."

She turns and looks at him.

"You must've missed that."

He shrugs.

"Anyway," Yarden says, "my mom has been going absolutely insane about it. She made us clean our rooms three times each, chose our outfits, has been cooking like crazy since yesterday..."

"I get it. She wants to show her man how nice and normal her family is."

"Funny," she says, rolling her eyes.

"Come on, you didn't act like this the first time you brought home Gal?"

"Not the same!"

"Why not?"

"Because Gal is my age! I'm supposed to be out dating and anyway...I cared more about preparing him for my family than vice versa."

Jeremy nods.

"Fair enough," he says. "Where is he anyway?"

"Gal? He's stuck on base this weekend. Somewhere near Gaza."

Yarden shoots Jeremy a grin.

"That's why I'm so glad you're here. I need somebody to whine to!"

"Great."

"Don't worry. I'll make sure you sit between me and Nof. We three will keep each other busy."

Jeremy's eyes shift down.

"Where is Nof?" he asks.

"I think mom asked her to run some errands. She'll be home soon. Why?"

"Just wondering," he says, raising his head. "Didn't get to say hello yet."

Yarden stops rummaging though her clothes and turns to stare at him, unblinking.

"I need to ask you something, Jeremy," she says. "Nof. You know that she—"

Ronit squawks out her name from the kitchen before Yarden can say another word. She groans.

"I'll be right back," she says. "Go ahead and shower and whatever. You look like you've been through hell."

She runs out. Left alone in the room, Jeremy exhales loudly. He'd been holding his breath again. He looks out Yarden's window, out at the hedges of oranges behind the house. He thinks of the chase. The sweat.

"Jeremy, meet Roger."

Jeremy would rather not meet Roger.

"So this is the 'adopted son' you've been telling me about!" Roger says, making quotations with his fat fingers. He spits when he talks. And talk he does.

"Yes, this is him," Ronit says, smiling at Roger expectantly. "Our soldier!"

Roger snatches Jeremy's hand and shakes it.

"The soldier!" Roger growls out, trying to intone the sound of machismo. "If I'd made *aliyah* twenty years earlier, I might have been a soldier too."

He still shakes Jeremy's hand.

"I'm not the only soldier," Jeremy reminds them. "Yarden has got a few months left of her service."

"Yes," Roger nods, "but you are the warrior, if I remember correctly!"

"Translated, sure," Jeremy says. "But that makes it sound a lot cooler than it is."

Roger releases Jeremy's hand and puts his arm around Ronit's shoulders.

"The whole family together!" he says.

Jeremy glances at Yarden, shaking her head in disbelief.

"No," Jeremy says. "You're forgetting Nof."

"Of course I am," Roger says. "Where is she?"

"She should be home any minute," Ronit says. "Let's sit down."

The men sit down at the table. Ronit and Yarden stand at the side, swirling their hands above the candles, singing softly. They finish and Jeremy recites the prayer over the wine and the bread. Rituals more of habit than need. Jeremy dips the challah into salt and passes it.

"So you're the man of the house, eh?" Roger asks him.

Jeremy opens his mouth to answer.

"How long have you been coming here now?" Roger goes on. "Since you started the army, I mean."

"Ronit has had me for over a year now."

"Your accent—you're from Cherry Hill, aren't you?"

"Nearby. Why? You also from Jersey?"

Roger ignores the question and presses on.

"Do you come home every weekend?" he asks. "You can't, I'm sure, being a paratrooper and all. You must be forced to spend some weekends on base."

"Most weekends I'm on base."

"Do you call Ronit your mother? I only ask because I have heard of lone soldiers, like you, who grow so close to their adopted families, that they call their moms 'Mom' and their brothers 'Brother' and their—"

"Sisters, 'Sister,'" Jeremy interrupts.

"That's right," Roger says. "So do you?"

Jeremy appraises him coolly. Yarden leans forward.

"Jeremy's like the brother we never had."

"That is precious," Roger says.

"He's always helping around," Yarden says. "Last week he fixed my shower curtains."

"Shower curtains!" Roger says. "So you're a handyman too, eh?"

"No, I specialize in curtains," Jeremy says. "You got any hobbies, Roger?"

Roger takes a deep breath. Jeremy kicks himself for asking. Then just as Roger begins to answer, the sound of the door opening and keys jangling stops him. They all look in the direction of the front door. Nof is home.

"Hi!" she yells out. "Sorry I'm late!"

She throws her purse on the couch, takes off her shoes, hopping, and ambles toward them. Her posture is bent. She is without grace, without one refined manner. Lazy and wild and alive. Jeremy watches her and tries to restrain what stirs within him. Still, his crooked mouth betrays his effort. Nof gets to the table and kisses Ronit on the cheek.

"Hi Mom," she says.

"Nof!" Roger exclaims.

"Roger," she says, nodding at him.

Nof passes Yarden, only stopping to squeeze her shoulder. Then she walks around the table to Jeremy and she grins.

"Been a while, Jeremy," she says. She leans in to hug him. It lasts a second too long. The scent of vanilla.

She stands up and walks to her chair.

"So," Nof says, "did I miss anything?"

They eat—all of them except for Roger, who is too busy digressing from one story or philosophy to the next. Now he's onto family values. Ronit watches him, smitten. Yarden texts her boyfriend. And Jeremy and Nof sit next to one another, passing back and forth her iPhone.

"So my point is," Roger says, pausing only to eat a potato, "that a family, a good family is a group of people who trust each other."

Nof types into the phone, "When will he shutt uuuup?"

Jeremy types back, "Never. The guy's a fucking energizer bunny."

"A what?" she writes.

"Nvm," he types.

"You don't even have to be related," Roger says. "I feel like I've had many families in my life. And in all of them, what we needed was this...this conviction in one another."

Jeremy writes, "He could be worse."

"Yeah right," Nof writes backs.

"He could be some *ars* from Afula."

Nof snorts and puts the phone in her lap. Then she picks it up and types.

"I don't know," she writes. "Americans are pretty bad too."

He raises his eyebrows at her. She cracks up.

"jk, jk," she writes, laughing.

"Trust," Roger says, "is the key. If I trust Ronit here and if she trusts me, then that's all the two of us need."

Roger looks into Ronit's eyes, all dewy-eyed. Nof looks into Jeremy's and does a mock noose with her hand above her head. They both try to stifle their laughter.

"But," Roger says, turning to look at Nof and Yarden and Jeremy, "a family isn't two people. It's more. I need to win your trust too."

Now Yarden looks up from her phone, looks right at Roger, and to his surprise what Jeremy sees in her usually steel gaze is something softer. Mild admiration. Jeremy glances at Nof to see if Roger's won her over too. Not so much.

"What is it?" Jeremy types into the phone.

Nof writes, "I hate this guy."

"Hey, at least he's nice, right? It seems like really likes your mom."

"I don't care," she writes. "It just pisses me off."

Now Jeremy actually speaks.

"What does?" he asks her.

She opens her mouth to respond, then looks in the direction of Roger, now describing his personal military theory, and stops. She types into the phone and passes it to him.

"He's a fucking intruder. He's not a part of this family. And he acts like he is."

Jeremy nods and looks down. He passes the phone back to her without responding. She looks at him and then shakes her head.

"I don't think that about you," she writes.

"No?"

"No. You're like a big brother to me."

Jeremy groans.

"lol. Okay. Not a brother. What do you want to hear?"

"I don't know," he writes.

Yarden's phone rings. She picks it up and walks out of the dining room. Nof looks over at her and then back at Jeremy.

"Do you think of me as a sister?" she writes into the phone.

"No."

"What about Yarden?"

"Yeah. She's like a sister."

"But not me?"

He shakes his head. Very calm.

"So what am I to you?" she writes.

He hesitates, his fingers floating above the glowing buttons of the iPhone.

"More," he writes.

She reads the phone and looks him in the eye and as she does, he feels her foot slide around his ankle. His hand—it crawls beneath the table to her right thigh. It climbs. She coughs and looks in the direction of Ronit and Roger.

"Mom," she says. "Can we be excused?"

Across the backyard they run, run to the periphery of their land, to the wooden fence and the weak board in it. Jeremy throws the flimsy wooden boards aside as Nof slips through the hole in the fence. He goes through after her. Walking ahead, she peers over her shoulder to make sure he's following. There is no moon this night. He is to her a dark shape and she the same to him.

"You see me?" she asks.

"I see the smile on your face," Jeremy says. "Your teeth."

Nof spins around and walks backward, away from him but facing him. She tries to stop her smile.

"Watch out," he says. "You might trip."

"Aw Jeremy," she sighs out in mock sentimentality, "you worried about me?"

"Must you be so ironic all the time?"

"You prefer me boring and normal?"

"I prefer—"

Nof yells out in surprise; the back of her right foot meets the protruding root of a tree. Jeremy, half ready, slide-tackles the dirt, falling under her thin frame just in time so that she collapses upon him. Her elbow stabs him right in the ribs.

"Jesus!" he says, gasping.

"Shit!" she shouts, "I'm so sorry! You alright?"

"I told you to be careful," he says. But he laughs.

She laughs too.

"You're right. You did," she says.

She puts her hand to his chest where he grips.

"Here?"

He nods. Nof pulls his hand away from the spot and bends her head down to it. She kisses it.

"There," she says. "All better."

"You're gonna have to do better than that."

She looks up at him from his chest. She finds the top button of the shirt and unbuttons it. She unbuttons the one below it and slides her hand across his flesh to the same injured spot.

"Getting warmer?" she asks.

"It's a start," Jeremy says and he pulls her face to his and kisses her.

Underneath the orange tree they lie. His hands stray about her every corner. Then his fingers duck down the front of her jeans.

"No," Nof suddenly whispers.

"What?" Jeremy asks, barely thinking.

"No," she says again.

"What do you mean, 'no'?"

She grabs his hands and stops kissing him. Teeth scrape against teeth.

"What is it?" he asks, impatient.

"This…" she says. "I can't."

"It's okay," Jeremy says, shaking his head. "I'll teach you."

"I don't want to learn."

He kisses her, close-mouthed.

"You want this," he says. "Why else would you flirt with me every time I'm home?"

He looks her in the eye.

"Why else would you take me here tonight?"

She opens her mouth to speak but says nothing.

"Tell me to stop," he says, "and I'll stop. Okay?"

Before she nods, before she lets him kiss her again, Jeremy sees in her expression terror. Terror not of the unknown. No, of the very much known, of the intimately known and forever dreaded. Even in the dark, it is unmistakable. He reads it in the screwed up corners of her eyes and in the shrink of her shoulders and for a second, he asks himself, what it is he's doing. Then he breathes in and he smells the scent of the oranges and under it, the hint of vanilla on her. He waits no longer; he acts and for one moment, just one, Jeremy reassures himself.

Dreams do come true.

They walk out of the grove together but apart. Nof is mute. He attempts to talk to her but her answer is silence. They walk along an aisle of the grove towards the only light, emanating from the hole in the wooden fence. Jeremy looks at the fence and he remembers the world before they crossed it, made up of taunts and trivial concerns and he feels a nostalgia for the lightness that world possessed though it only changed that very night. Jeremy knows Nof will never speak to him again, for when she did cry out, did he hear her?

She slips through the fence and walks toward the house. He stands on the other side for a moment, the wind-tussled trees his only company. He watches her open the door and enter. And then he follows her himself.

When Jeremy enters the kitchen, expecting to see Nof there, he is instead greeted by Roger, alone.

"Sit down, warrior!" he yells out, all cheery and wine-addled. It makes Jeremy jump anyway.

"What?" Jeremy asks, looking toward the hallway for a sign of Nof or Yarden or Ronit.

"Come on," Roger says. "Sit with me."

Jeremy sits. He glances again at the hallway, nervous who might come out, nervous what they might know.

"Tell me something…" Roger whispers. "How did you get so lucky?"

Jeremy turns his attention to Roger, "What do you mean?"

"This family. How did you end up with them?"

"I met Yarden in an army course," Jeremy says. "We became friends. She invited me over for Shabbat dinner and…"

"And that was that! They adopted you!" Roger says.

"No," Jeremy says, shaking his head. "No. Not at all. After what they've been through, the women in this house…No. It was not so simple."

Jeremy looks down the hallway again. He listens for the sound that might affirm his fears, maybe of Nof crying to her mother. Maybe of Nof whispering to Yarden. A part of him wishes he would hear it. He turns back to Roger.

"You think you can win them over with compliments and smart speeches?" Jeremy asks. "You think that impresses them at all? Maybe you've fooled Ronit but the girls…they're not suckers."

"What?!" Roger says, taken aback. "You make it sound like I'm some con artist!"

"Well, aren't you?!" Jeremy says, teeth clenched. "Isn't that exactly what it's all about? You're not here for the girls. You are here for Ronit. And all that Yarden and Nof are is in the way of your goal, which is to fuck their mom."

"You're wrong, Jeremy," Roger says quietly. "That's not it at all."

"No?!" Jeremy shouts. "So set it straight!"

For once, Roger is quiet. He looks at Jeremy, looks him up and down and then he speaks.

"You say that I'm after Ronit," Roger says, "like it's a game. Like I'm out for the hunt. But I don't have that in me, Jeremy. To lie...to calculate it all like that? No."

Roger takes a deep breath.

"I can see why you might see it that way, at your age. But what I want... it's not just Ronit. It's to be a part of her life. The same way you are."

Jeremy cannot bear it. This man, he's too sincere to take. He burrows his gaze into the ground.

"You've been blessed," Roger says. "I mean, blessed to be a part of a family like this. To have them call you brother and son. I'm sure that's why you're so hostile toward me. You're worried I'm going to hurt them. But listen."

Roger leans in and puts a hand on Jeremy's shoulder.

"I won't lie to you. Ronit's kids? They come with the package, whether I like it or not. But I want to do right this time. I want to try and get to know them. That means you too."

Jeremy breathes long ragged breaths.

"You'll never be one of them," Jeremy whispers. "They will never let you in completely."

"Then I'll get as close as I can."

Jeremy looks up into the eyes of Roger. Roger's hand still lies upon his shoulder, his arm drawn out straight, facing Jeremy like an empty highway.

158

"You're for real, aren't you?" Jeremy asks. His voice cracks.

"I hope so," Roger answers.

A door opens in the hallway and Roger lets go of Jeremy's shoulder. Ronit walks over to the table. Jeremy does not look up at her. He cannot bear the sight.

"Jeremy," she says.

"Yes?"

"Can I get you some desert?"

Now Jeremy looks up at Ronit, at her smiling face and he tries to moves his mouth. He forces its corners to stand, makes himself smile just once more. For her. For all of them.

"No, Ronit," he says. "I think I'd burst."

TAL TOLEDANO

When Tal Toledano told a joke, everybody—even the mefaked—laughed.

He assumed, like the whole lot of Ashkenazi soldiers, intellectual superiority on every subject. But this Ashkenazi-born confidence, fused with the mad Moroccan blood he had inherited, made Toledano in the eyes of Confinement Base 394's denizens, an extraordinary specimen of soldier, let alone prisoner.

A true mutt, Toledano wore his olive-colored skin like a medal of honor. He quickly galvanized the military prison's Mizrahi gangs with his Moroccan heritage and soft-pedaled the ostentatious white kids with his articulate tongue. He told the meanest jokes, sparing neither side their idiosyncrasies.

"What do you call a Yemenite speaking Yiddish?" Toledano once asked us, standing in the compound's patchy courtyard during our fifteen-minute window of free time.

We stared at him blankly. Somebody asked, "What?"

"A sh-megeggy-arabi."

I could have told the same joke to the applause of crickets. Toledano received whoops and guffaws and a standing ovation. He had that intense effect upon people, all people. In prison, outside—it made no difference. Charm can take a man a long way no matter where he stands.

Yes, Toledano changed Base 394. I wish I could tell you I was his friend, his closest pal. But when you've got a name like mine, Schnitzer, you are branded Ashkenazi and it's left at that.

Toledano once told me, "Schnitzer, you're a great kid. But I can't pick you over Tubol. I can't pick Oshri over Igor. That's the way this place works."

He was too busy being an entertainer to be a real friend to anybody. Maybe that was his curse.

Before Tal Toledano, Confinement Base 394 resembled most military prisons. Soldiers loitered around for a week, a month, sometimes a year. They trickled in and out without leaving a single imprint on any body or thing. They meant as much to one another as the rags they wore.

As for the offences that had landed them in prison, these varied from soldier to soldier. Violence was the most popular crime. One kid claimed he had threatened to murder his entire platoon. Another claimed he had gone further than threaten. Rumor had it that one soldier had raped a young girl. And then there had been Abel, the giant American who had broken every rule the book had to offer. Nobody missed him much.

The base harbored 600 such prisoners at a time, a ragtag batch of reject soldiers dividing themselves up into posses. The common religions and races found each other, as they always do, fudging some semblance of solidarity.

The Russians, Ukrainians and other Slavs occupied the East fences, chain-smoking cigarettes and whining about their homelands with pseudo-nostalgia. The Ethiopians owned the one patch of grass in an otherwise barren courtyard. Sometimes they'd pitch an impromptu soccer game with a tennis ball.

The Ashkenazi kids controlled the "library," a mere shelf in an empty storage closet, and the laundry, propagating the influx of illicit goods. Their typical merchandise: cigarettes, porn, and the occasional knife.

The Ashkenazim were known as the heady kids, the readers, dreamers and poets – the pretentious dicks. And I was one of them.

The kitchen and bench press were Mizrahi territory. They, the children of Moroccan, Yemenite, Iraqi, and other Arab lineage were the largest clan on Base 394. Within the clique were sub-cliques and sub-cliques within those.

In between cooking dishes like *bourekas* and *shakshuka*, the Mizrahi cooks played backgammon. This was their game, a sacred and discriminatory game no non-Mizrahi soul dared to attempt, lest he wish to lose a hand. They ruled the dice. They over-spiced the soup to piss off the Ashkenazi soldiers. They got into brutal fistfights with each other and almost masochistically went about realizing every cliché of the *ars* stigma.

The Ashkenazim and Mizrahim were, to the military officers of Confinement Base 394, the most consistently unruly and unpleasant batch of Israeli soldiers the prison had to offer.

Nobody could tame them. That is, until Tal Toledano came to town.

There are, to this day, a great number of competing mythologies, regarding the story of Toledano's origin.

Some claim he assaulted a Krav Maga instructor. Others say he tested positive in a drug test. The most romantic tale supposes that Toledano did no more than stand up to a power-hungry mefaked. Toledano neither corroborated nor denied a single story. What I do know is that he arrived on a Wednesday morning, shared his cell with a gloomy American kid named Berman, and three months later left Confinement Base 394 and never returned.

As for how he spent those three months, Toledano did not merely pacify one posse. He courted the prison's two greatest cliques, the Ashkenazim and Mizrahim, and then proceeded to blur the lines between us. We found ourselves laughing at the same jokes, often at our own expense. More importantly, he appealed to our common impulses.

I remember one morning, Toledano gathered up as many soldiers as he could find during the recess. Ashkenazim and Mizrahim—we were all intermingled. He told us to all come in tight and to listen closely.

"Listen," he said, his face serious and his tone low and solemn. "I have some very pressing business to discuss with you."

Everyone shut up and watched Toledano, entranced. He grabbed a short white kid, with a face about as pretty as a burst pimple, by the neck and pulled him to the middle.

"This is Oded," he said. "Everybody say, 'Hi Oded.'"

We glanced at each other and shrugged and repeated the words. "Hi Oded," we said in grumbled unison.

"Little Oded, here," Toledano continued, "is a virgin."

Some people snorted and began to laugh and Toledano glared at them. One of them, he addressed specifically.

"Shut it, Nadav!" he said. "We all know which way you lean."

After some amused chatter, we all quieted down again and listened to Toledano.

"As you know," he said, "tomorrow is Visitor's Day. Now, I've pulled some strings to get Oded a very particular type of visitor...if you know what I mean."

At this, everyone began to whisper in disbelieving awe.

"Shush!" Toledano exclaimed. "Keep it low. This is the plan."

So it happened that Tal Toledano sequestered a holding cell during the 30-minute window of visiting hours, brought a prostitute to Confinement Base 394 and, with our help, snuck her and Oded into the cell together. While the little Ashkenazi kid lost his virginity, two Mizrahim stood outside the room guarding. This was the first of Toledano's many wonders.

Soon, a Polish kid named Levenschtein won a backgammon tournament. For an Ashkenazi to play, let alone win, a backgammon game was big news. Another soldier named Damari, of Iraqi origin, discovered a sudden fondness for poetry and began to work in the library. A Mizrahi waxing intellectual seemed even odder. Toledano shook every convention and certainty of the Prison to its core.

Toledano even won over the warden of the prison, the so-called mem pay. He visited his offices on multiple occasions and, while most soldiers would normally sneer at such activity and call Toledano a *malamnik*, even the most bitter and despondent prisoners seemed incapable of criticizing Toledano. After each of Toledano's visits, the mem pay allowed longer recesses, delivered a variety of spices to the kitchen, and expanded the library from one shelf to two.

Toledano made Base 394 so bearable that some active soldiers began to disobey their orders just to end up there. If this sounds unreasonable, keep in mind that guard duty is not so different from imprisonment. Toledano narrowed this difference to the extent of his capability.

Then one day, I saw him come very close to tears. This was the first and only time I recollect the shadow of melancholy on Toledano's face.

A fight broke out between his roommate Berman and a Russian prisoner. The Russian drew a knife. Toledano attempted to mollify both sides before any serious damage could be done and in the tussle the Russian almost sliced off his finger. Berman ended up with the blade in his gut just as the mefakedim arrived.

Two of them grabbed the Russian. Three others gathered around Berman's limp body. Restrained by the guards, the Russian screamed out to Toledano, "We're not your fucking toys. Stop playing us!"

Toledano's face changed. His mouth opened to respond and then closed. His eyes darted back and forth from Berman, being carted away, to the Russian, being dragged. His eyes watered but he did not cry.

Toledano looked down and walked away from the scene. And I followed him.

He sat in his cell on Berman's bed. He glanced at me as I entered and then looked away. I did not want to disturb him, so I waited at the edge of the wall until he spoke.

"I wish there was some Russian in me," he said, almost whispering.

I asked him why.

"Some American too," he said, not to me. "Some Ethiopian. Some French…"

I tried to comfort Toledano. I pleaded against his conviction that the fight was his fault. But he just stared into space, listing off ethnicities. He seemed, in that moment, lost in a bereft trance.

Later I would come to understand. Toledano could help the Mizrahim and the Ashkenazim get along because he was like them. He shared their blood. But the rest shared no ancestry with Toledano, and thus owed him no allegiance. He could play nice all he liked. But the Russians, the Ethiopians, and the others on Confinement Base 394, would never honor the persuasions of a half-Mizrahi, half-Ashkenazi soldier.

For the first time, Tal Toledano understood the extent and limitations of his influence. His severed finger remained a lasting and painful reminder.

One week later, Berman returned to the prison, bandaged but otherwise okay. Then after a few days, the prison released his beloved cellmate, who returned to his company stationed on a kibbutz near the Gaza Strip.

That is all that is known of Tal Toledano. When he left, the populace of the prison once again divided into its ethnic cliques. The mefakedim tightened the rules back to the pre-Toledano levels and life on Confinement Base 394 resumed as it was before the arrival of that peculiar soldier.

But, like graffiti on a wall, I hear that some vestiges of Toledano still remain.

Once a month, the prisoners hold backgammon tournaments. And no one can remember the last time a Mizrahi kid won.

OPERATION GET SOME: PART III

The words began as whispers. The freshman students spoke of the room on the second floor of Rieber Residence Hall with mingled suspicion and intrigue. They said the walls were covered with hand-woven tapestries, the floors with rugs and throw pillows. Colored keffiyehs supposedly decorated the center table upon which stood a hookah, and Middle Eastern music wailed from a set of knock-off speakers.

As for the room's sole inhabitant, the few witnesses said he was an older guy with an odd accent and a penchant for tight jeans. Whether he was an Arab or a Persian or a Turk was of great dispute among the sons and daughters of such cultures. Nobody knew his name, not yet.

It was, after all, the first day of college. Nobody knew anybody's name.

But at UCLA, news travels fast and before long, two girls came to knock upon the enigmatic foreigner's door to settle the rumors once and for all.

They knocked. The door opened and there he stood, eyeing them with a pair of wild orange eyes and smiling his crooked smile.

"Hello," Yoav said to the two blonde bombshells. "Want to come in?"

To be fair, the ex-Israeli soldier's room did contain a fair amount of Arab adornments. However, the little birds had omitted one particular detail of the room: a massive Israeli flag pinned to the ceiling.

Yoav took great pleasure in the decoration of his harem. He could not believe the day had come. The student-visa and acceptance letter to UCLA had finally paid off. As of today, he was officially an enrolled mathematics student, residing in a dorm with a bunch of 18-year-old American kids.

America. Oh, how Yoav loved this "land of opportunity," a phrase he found ripe with innuendo. In the few short weeks he had spent in Los Angeles, Yoav had already met a dozen young Jewish girls and deflowered half of them.

This, compared to Israel, where getting lucky meant getting kissed. On the cheek. Yoav thanked the day he had cut his Army ID, given away his uniform, signed the release papers, and walked away from the military base a free man. Only two days later, he had hopped on a flight aimed for Los Angeles with the intent of never looking back.

And yet, Yoav felt strange. When he had given his gun, the one he called Luck, back to the armory, he had acted without a slip of hesitancy. But now he found that he missed Luck, missed the feel of her cold metal on his fingertips and her weight upon his shoulder. He felt defenseless and naked without her.

And he thought too of his old American friend, Aaron Klotsky, whom he had left in Israel without so much as a text of farewell.

Nevermind, he thought to himself. *You're the one in America now.*

"So, do you have, like, PTSD or something?"

This was a first.

"PTSD?" he asked.

"Y'know," the little ginger girl stammered. "Post trauma something something disorder?"

"You say 'something' a lot."

At this, the girl laughed. "I've been told that a lot!"

Yoav nodded his head, simultaneously amused and irritated.

This was the speed-dating icebreaker. The students stood outside Royce Hall, split up into randomly assigned groups. In two lines, they faced each other. One shifted left every sixty seconds. The purpose of the game was to make friends, no doubt. Yoav, however, had other plans.

"What are you doing tonight?" he asked the ginger, who was cute despite her red condition and idiotic questions.

"Tonight?" she asked.

"Come over to Rieber, level two, room 134. I'm throwing a little freshman mixer."

He said this to every girl he met in line, figuring that 10% would actually show. He would impress them with his army stories, his dog tags, and worn beret. He would speak of his service in casual terms and avoid all sober talk. His so-called PTSD would not make the cut.

A girl clapped her hands. It was the bubbly junior in charge of the icebreaker.

"Okay, everybody!" she yelled out. "Switch again!"

Yoav shifted his feet and his gaze toward his new partner. Unfortunately a male.

"Hi," the kid said.

Yoav nodded at him, disinterested.

"You're the army guy, right?"

Again, Yoav nodded.

"Wow! That's pretty sick. Did you...uh...did you kill anybody over there?"

Yoav blinked and looked at the kid.

"What?" he asked, bewildered.

"Did you—"

"I heard you the first time," Yoav interrupted him. "What is *with* you kids?"

The boy frowned. "What do you mean?"

"Did I kill anybody? What the fuck kind of question is that?"

The kid nearly trembled. A couple other students stopped small-talking to turn and stare at Yoav. He hesitated.

"You all want to know if I killed somebody?"

Three kids nodded, including his partner. Yoav almost laughed but instead he stooped down and shadowed his expression.

"Yeah," he said, lowering his voice in mock grandiosity. "I killed a terrorist every day of the week."

All the children, for they truly were children, gaped at him, horrified. Almost all of them, anyway. One girl at the end of the line suddenly snorted and burst into laughter. Yoav could hardly see her. Everybody turned toward her now.

"Why are you laughing?" one girl asked, all staccato and good diction.

"Cause he's messing with you!" Yoav heard the girl exclaim.

He smiled. Staccato girl said, "No! No, he is not!"

"Eh…" Yoav began, "I am, actually."

Now, the lines parted and in between them, Yoav could see the girl at the end. She was a blonde, yes, but by no means a beauty. Perhaps, you could call her cute. Yoav disagreed with her dimples, her disheveled hair and dark brown eyes. But her knowing smile reminded him of somebody, a girl he had known long ago and never ventured to meet again. He shuddered at the thought. Annabelle.

Like Annabelle, this girl impressed Yoav with the physicality of her intelligence. But Yoav did not intend to make the same mistake twice.

The kids turned toward Yoav again and his partner appeared offended.

"How could you make a joke like that?" he asked.

This time, Yoav burst into laughter, shaking his head. And faintly, he recognized that only one other person laughed along with him.

Within two weeks, the rumors surrounding the enigmatic ex-Israeli soldier spread to every corner of the campus. He attended one Hillel event and left with more phone numbers than he had fingers. He flirted with AEPi and a few other Jewish fraternities during their rush events, but left unimpressed. He appeared indifferent to the rare ethical query regarding his philandering ways with girls four years his junior.

To some, he was a creep. To others, a champion. But to everybody, he was *that guy*. *That guy*, the legal twenty-one year-old living in the dorms and, by proxy, the freshman class's alcohol dispenser. Yes, Yoav sold so many handles, fifths, and water bottles full of spirits, he reckoned that by December he'd be able to pay off the majority of his student loans.

Yoav rapidly became the most popular student in all of Rieber Hall for this very reason and yet somehow, despite all the attention, the countless girls and flowing liquor, Yoav felt hollow.

He told himself to quit being a bitch, to man up and to enjoy college. But somewhere between the ribs and the atriums of his heart, in the confines there he sensed a profound and terrible emptiness. This was more than the mere ennui of an overindulged college student. Much worse. This was loneliness. He could buy himself all the false friends in the world, fuck to his dick's content as many loose American girls as he pleased—he remained, despite every appearance to the contrary, alone.

So he learned to act like an American, to architect a grand façade and refuse the admission of any feeling. And the students loved him for the mysteries his soul harbored.

One night in a drunk stupor, Yoav stumbled into his room, sat down at his laptop, logged into Skype and saw Aaron Klotsky's name highlighted in green. His old friend was online. He dragged his finger along the trackpad, moving the cursor toward the "call" button and stopped. Even in this state, he knew it was a bad idea. He did not want to indulge in nostalgia. Plus, he had plenty of new friends.

But Yoav knew that Aaron Klotsky would never call to ask a favor. He would never pay Yoav to buy him liquor and call him the "coolest". Aaron was better than these see-through college kids, these white cookie cutter suburb pricks. Aaron actually knew him.

With these thoughts present, Yoav pressed the button. The digital phone rang once. Twice. Three times and then Yoav hung up. *It was a stupid idea anyway,* he told himself and he shut the laptop closed.

The Professor was a hipster. Or so he wished, anyway. Yoav sat in a modern philosophy class a few weeks later, eyeing the young, recently PhD'd instructor with utter contempt.

He wore a sweater vest, corduroys, a perma-sardonic smile and Lacoste slip-ons. He spoke with a voice at once superior and self-conscious, and seemed, to Yoav, the epitome of insincere and stupid.

The Professor was America at its worst. But to Yoav's delight, it turned out the Professor's critics were more than one. Sitting in the back of the classroom, Yoav saw a hand rise above the crowd and heard a voice speak and he recognized her instantly.

"Ms. Miller, is it?" asked the Professor.

"Yeah," she said. "Liana."

He could see only her hair, the same blonde spaghetti mess of curls and he smiled, despite himself. *So her name's Liana*, Yoav thought. *Liana Miller.*

"Right, Liana," the Professor said. "What do you think Montaigne is trying to say here?"

She hesitated a moment, digging a strand of hair behind her ear.

"I think…" she said, "I think he's pissed off."

The Professor raised his eyebrows and smiled a big, beautiful condescending smile.

"Well," he said, "that sure is the tip of the iceberg. But—"

"Hey—" she said, "I didn't finish."

It was as if she'd slapped the Professor across the face; he appeared completely floored. The class erupted into manic whispers, the students invigorated by this girl's sudden unforeseen nerve. The Professor frowned but then nodded and forced a smile.

"Okay Liana," he said. "Enlighten us."

Liana straightened her back and sat upright, while Yoav scooted forward to the edge of his seat, an intrigued smile spread across his lips. He looked forward to this.

"I think Montaigne is pissed off at people," she said. "I mean, stupid people. He mostly talks about the religious and how they claim certainty on God, on morality. But it's not just them. It's everybody! Everybody claims they know everything. People got all the answers. But there's that line in *Raymond Sebond*. He said..."

She looked down at her notes for a moment and then back up at the Professor.

"He said, 'What do I know?' Is that not the most humble thing you've ever heard? I mean, for a philosopher to say 'What the hell do I know?'"

Yoav watched as each syllable poured from her mouth more pronounced than the next. He marveled at the severity of her speech, artless and yet full of a stilted sort of insight. He wondered what minds had come together to copulate and spur this little blonde head-case into being. Yoav very much admired her parentage.

"Montaigne," Liana continued. "He's not forcing some philosophy down our throats. He's okay with doubt. His faith *is* uncertainty. Isn't that crazy?"

She looked expectantly around at her classmates, most of who had zoned out after her first sentence. *Shallow little shits*, Yoav thought. As for the Professor, he hesitated for a moment, his hands clasped together. Then the fingers unlocked and the wobbly mouth opened.

"You make an interesting point," the Professor said. "But I do not find any evidence that he is so *disappointed*. Maybe he is indeed *critical* of people. But Montaigne is too complex to merely pigeonhole one way or another. Let's try and read this from a literary critic's perspective. Here..."

Yoav paid him no more heed. Instead he watched as the girl shook her head. He saw her collapse into her arms, disinterested. It appeared, from Yoav's vantage point, if the Professor did not intend to listen to Liana, she would not hear him either.

He liked her. Yoav could sense his attraction to her, to her intelligence, and it worried the holy hell out of him. Annabelle had played him. Would Liana Miller do the same? After some spirited debate between his prick and his pride, he decided he would rather not find out.

When the lecture ended and students began to pack up their bags, Yoav hastened to exit the classroom so as not to meet Liana again. He walked past the desks, leaned his hand toward the handle and saw another hand touch it first. Too late.

Liana looked up at him, there at the threshold of the classroom and hallway, and she smirked.

"You," she said. "I remember you."

Yoav smiled faintly and nodded toward the door.

"You leaving?" he asked.

"Yeah," she said, turning the handle. "Sure."

She pushed open the door and allowed Yoav out. For a second he considered storming off right there, but instead he turned to hold the door open for her. *These Americans are rubbing off on me,* he thought, cursing his own chivalry.

"Thanks," she said.

She pulled the strap of her backpack over her shoulder and passed through the doorway. He let the door go and together they walked through the hallway toward the stairs. They were quiet. He peered at her from the corner of his eye and saw the hint of a smile on her lips.

"What?" he asked her.

"Nothing," she said, holding her laughter.

"Is it about class? I mean, that Professor—"

"Nope, not about that."

And now she laughed out loud.

"Okay," he said, nodding impatiently. "Can I get a hint?"

"No, that's no fun."

He shook his head. "Sorry, I don't play these games. Where I'm from, Israel, people are straight—"

"Forward?" she again interrupted. "You talk too slow. I'll tell you."

They came to the end of the hallway and this time when Yoav pushed the door open, Liana held the door ajar for him.

"Thanks," he said under his breath.

"Listen," she said, "you've got a name."

"A name?"

"Yeah, a nickname. A pseudonym. An alias, y'know?"

"What name?" Yoav asked.

"They call you…"

She burst out into laughter, calmed down and then spoke in a low voice.

"They call you the Prophet."

"The…the what?!"

"I know! I heard about it from my roommate."

Yoav furrowed his brow.

"Who…why?" he asked. "What's with that? The Prophet?"

"Yeah, apparently because you're an Arab."

"I'm not—"

"And cause you buy everybody alcohol," she continued. "They call it 'delivering your *sermon*.'"

She made her fingers quotations for that last word.

"I don't know what you're talking about," Yoav tried.

"You serious, Yoav?" she asked. "You think I don't know? Everybody knows you sell."

Yoav glared at her, assessing her candor. Then, convinced, he shook his head in exasperation.

"Great," he said, deadpan. "Just what I need. More publicity."

"I think it's kinda cool," she said. "If I were you, I'd capitalize on the fame."

"Yeah? You're just full of ideas, aren't you?"

She turned and stared at him. "You have no idea."

So he'd broken his self-made promise. So what? Liana was attractive, clever, and best of all, emotionally detached. In their ensuing conversation through the Luvalle Commons, past the Dickson Plaza and discontinued at her destination, Perloff Hall, he had come to understand that Liana was fuck-buddy material, no more. She had, from what Yoav could tell, the heart of a jellyfish, the conscience of a killer, and a sense of humor so mean, it'd make an Israeli comedian blush.

But best of all, Liana was not Annabelle. Yoav could barely distinguish what characteristic he had believed they shared. Annabelle had been that rare impossible beauty and thus (naturally) a manipulative bitch. Liana on the other hand...well, the truth is, he did not know. She intrigued and repulsed him. She seemed irrevocably bland one second and startlingly beautiful the next. She was contrast in and of itself. And for the briefest moment, she had made Yoav feel a little less alone.

He decided he would indulge himself just this once. They had planned to meet that evening at a taco-truck parked near the Court of Sciences. As all these ruminations rushed through his mind, Yoav walked in the direction of his dorm. When his phone rang, he answered it absent-mindedly.

"Hello?" he said without even glancing at the caller ID.

"Yoav?" a familiar voice answered.

Yoav stopped dead in his tracks. "...Aaron?!"

"Yeah!" Aaron Klotsky exclaimed. "I finally got ahold of you!"

Yoav stopped and looked at his phone, amazed. He brought it back to his ear.

"Holy shit, Aaron," Yoav said, beginning to walk again, his eyes to the ground. "It's been a while."

"Sure has. How's my homeland treating you?"

"Good. Very good."

"You miss me?"

Yoav grunted. "Where..." he began. "Are you calling from Israel? This must cost you a fortune."

"Did you not see the number?"

"No, why?"

"Yoav," Aaron said, laughing. "Look up."

Yoav raised his eyes from the floor toward Rieber Residence Hall's entrance. Aaron Klotsky stood outside, a grin on his face and a girl by his side.

"Son of a bitch," Yoav mumbled, lowering the phone from his gob-smacked face.

Aaron ran up to Yoav, wrapped him in a bear hug and spun him around. They laughed and slapped each other in the face. Yoav punched Aaron hard in the gut and he kneeled over, wincing.

"You little shit," Aaron laughed.

"You didn't even send me an email to warn me?" Yoav asked, grinning. "You don't change, Klotsky."

Aaron stood up, raised his fists in jest and then glanced over at the girl beside him. He lowered his fists, rearranged his childish mien and stood up straight. Yoav gave her a quick once-over and immediately recognized a fellow Israeli. The corners and lines of her face were cut more jagged than a serrated knife. Her skin was olive and her feet wore Naot sandals.

He put two and two together before Aaron Klotsky could even open his mouth. She had come to California with Aaron. They had travelled together. They were serious. And clearly she had Aaron whipped worse than a full can of frosting. But worst of all, the very worst, she wore a ring around her finger.

Aaron began, "Let me introduce you to my—"

"Holy shit!" Yoav burst out.

He stared at her. Then at Aaron. Then at her.

"You're getting married?!" Yoav yelled out.

Aaron Klotsky opened his mouth to respond and then closed it. He saw the shock and anger swimming in his old friend's eyes and he knew no response. He looked at his fiancée for support and then tried a smile.

"Yeah, Yoav," Aaron said. "This March. In Tel Aviv."

Yoav's mouth hung there agape. He closed it and attempted to formulate a sentence in his head. He hated Aaron Klotsky in that moment. He wanted to scream at him, call him fool, call him sucker. He wanted to shake the living shit out of his friend, but instead he nodded.

"Wow," Yoav said. "I mean...wow!"

He hesitated a moment, looking at Aaron's feet. Then he raised his eyes. "Mazel tov."

Yoav knew he could have tried harder to make those last words sound sincere, but he could only fake so many American traits a day. The duplicitous smile was asking too much.

"Thanks," Aaron said, his voice strained. His eyes looked pained and his voice quavered a bit. "We're in California to meet my biological parents. I don't know if I ever told you—I'm adopted. My real parents, they're from Sherman Oaks."

Yoav nodded. This revelation might have once astonished him. But now it seemed downright petty next to that shining diamond on the girl's finger.

Yoav looked at her. He looked a little more closely and saw she was stunning, a true one-of-a-kind gorgeous. Like Annabelle. More like Anabelle than Liana could ever be. And he pitied his friend for a moment, knowing he'd suffer the rest of his life if he married her. But maybe American guys like their girls cold and rigid and asexual. Maybe she's everything Aaron Klotsky ever wanted.

Yoav stood there, lost in thought for a moment. Then he looked up, he took a step toward the girl and he held out his hand.

"Hi," he said in Hebrew. "It's nice to meet you."

And Yoav forced himself to smile.

Yoav said goodbye to his friend Aaron Klotsky with a bittersweet, awkward embrace. It lasted a few seconds too long as if it was the last hug the two friends would ever share. Afterward, he turned around and walked into his dorm without looking back. They had invited him to the wedding, of course. They had reminded him that if he couldn't make it, they were planning a second reception in California, down in Aaron's childhood home of La Jolla. Like hell, Yoav would attend. He wanted to be nowhere near Israel, near La Jolla, near Aaron Klotsky nor especially that Israeli piece of work he called a fiancée.

He took a cold shower to clear his mind of the encounter. He got dressed without too much fuss, combed his hair and walked out the door. He arrived fifteen minutes early to the Court of Sciences without even noticing it. When he checked his watch and realized his mistake, it was already too late. Liana had arrived early too.

"Hey Prophet," she said, smiling. "You're punctual."

Damn it, he thought. *First step of the operation. Always arrive late.*

"Yeah," he said. "Guess I'm hungry."

She stopped and screwed up her eyes and stared at him.

"You alright?"

"Fine."

"You look…off."

"Liana," he said, rolling his eyes. "Do you really care?"

"Mmmm—no," she said, conceding. "Not really."

"Good," he said and he laughed with relief.

He was in no mood to discuss Aaron Klotsky or the imminent marriage. He did not want to waste any of their time getting deep. No, Yoav wanted one thing and one thing only.

"Shall we?" she asked, nodding toward the food trucks.

"Yeah," he said. "Let's."

Those dimples were misleading, alright. Three hours, five tacos, and ten shots of tequila later, Yoav and Liana burst into Yoav's single room, tongue intertwined, hands reconnoitering each other's every curve and corner. They collapsed onto his bed and, without any pretense, began to tear each other's clothes off. By accident, they ripped down one of his Arab tapestries to the floor. She bit hard upon his clavicle and scratched against his sides and gripped the skin of his shoulders until he bruised. She was feisty; Yoav liked that.

He did not, however, enjoy the quantity he had allowed himself to drink. Yoav was more inebriated than he'd been in years. Another rule broken. It was as if, in response to the news of Aaron Klotsky's engagement, he had attempted to disregard every smooth move his mentor ever taught him. He wanted nothing to do with the old procedure, the proselyting of a fallen idol. No, the truth is Yoav was straight up sick of Operation Get Some. It had served him well during his military service, when on a daily basis he'd been restricted all access to ass.

But now Yoav was a free man. It was about time he started to act like one. Tonight with Liana, he had played the game differently. Gone were the lies, the backhanded insults, the manipulative wordplay and subtle obscenity. But the most distinct absence of all was Yoav's patience. He had made it very clear very early on to Liana: he wanted her now.

She had accommodated this wish with great gusto. Despite his insistence, she had drunk very little and merely watched, amused and sardonic, as he took shot after shot. And now he felt as if he'd drowned himself. Yoav could barely see straight.

He attempted to unclip the clasp of her bra strap with one hand and failed. He tried with two fumbling hands, failed again.

"Here," she said. "Let me help you."

This was a nightmare. He kissed her neck and she stopped him, calling it a pet peeve. He played the piano up her spine and she burst into laughter. *Ticklish*, he thought. *Great.* His attempts to be seductive or sexy, Liana outright mocked. He couldn't blame her there—he could hear himself slurring every word.

He felt her hand slither down his pants and thanked God that she was taking the initiative. She kissed him and caressed him and he lay there, slack. He wondered how she could even find him attractive in this state. And that's when she said it.

"Yoav," she whispered.

"Yeah?" he asked back, all breathy.

"You alright?"

"Yeah, why?"

"Uh…"

She hesitated, a small impenetrable smile on her lips.

"Wha—what now?" he asked.

"Well…I don't know how to say this."

"What?"

"You're not working," she said.

He stared at her for a second there in the dark of his dorm room, confused. And then it clicked. *Oh my god,* he whispered to himself. A horror more profound than any he'd ever suffered in his three years in the Israeli military, a humiliation worse than Annabelle, worse than any he'd ever known suddenly swallowed Yoav whole.

"Oh my god," he whispered again out loud.

Liana looked like she was about to burst. He lay there, aghast. Mortified and defeated.

"It's not so bad," she tried.

And then he looked at her, looked at the twitching corners of her mouth and he decided. He had to laugh.

It was forced at first, beginning softly as a husky repetitive breath. It grew into a high-pitched disbelieving inhalation. And then, without warning, Yoav sat up forward and burst out into the most thunderous laughter. His eyes stung with ashamed and regaled tears. Liana laughed too but quieter; she put her arms around his bare shoulders and her face to his back. He hyperventilated and gasped as she just sat there giggling, petting his chest with the tips of her fingers.

"Liana," he said in between gulps of air, "I—"

"Shut up," she said.

And now she took his face in her hands and she kissed him on the lips. He stopped shaking; he kissed her too. It was tender and forthright and honest. It shocked Yoav, more even than the night's liquor-induced short-comings.

He felt sympathy in that kiss. He felt longing. And he realized how misled Liana had left him with her brash jokes, irony and steely intelligence. He had said it himself: she was contrast. And this was the greatest contrast of all—this warmth, this unabashed caring. Liana Miller was chock full of surprises.

One of the tears on Yoav's cheek trickled down onto their lips. He could taste the salt. She pulled away from him and lay down upon his bed, watching him. He followed her, lying down himself. He looked back at her.

"This was unexpected," he said.

"I know," she said. "I thought you were supposed to be a player."

"No, a prophet."

"You saw this coming, did you?"

He shook his head and they both laughed again.

"Whiskey dick," he said. "I guess there's a first time for everything."

"Sure is," she said.

She kissed him again. And then they spoke. They spent the whole night speaking and listening to one another's stories, full of laughter and melancholy, so often intermingled. She spoke of Seattle, of how much smaller it seemed than Los Angeles. He spoke of Israel and the army. He spared her the shallow shit he had used so often to impress college girls. He spoke to her instead of the unimpressive, the ugly glossless stories, the kind that had left Yoav feeling numb. And she listened. She spoke of her sisters back home and he enquired over their quirks.

He told her of his brothers, of Schnitzer and Udi and Tooke and Abel and Gal and Jeremy Berman and Tal Toledano and Doron Levi and, of course, Aaron Klotsky. He told her about all the others soldiers he had left behind in that country and of his beloved M-16, Luck. And here and there she asked him questions to fill in the blanks or to translate a word she did not understand.

Minutes became hours, as the smoggy L.A. sky faded into a tinged royal blue. At one point he whispered into her ear a question. And she answered just as quietly, "Yes." They spoke for a few minutes longer until finally she fell asleep mid-sentence and he too closed his eyes.

Yoav awoke and the girl was gone. He gazed around his room for a second, his thought process muddied by a most hostile hangover. Then slowly he sat up, moaning and rubbing his eyes. He needed to piece the evening back together. He vaguely recollected Liana telling him she had an early class that morning. Thus her absence, he presumed. He could see the impression she had left on his bed, the tapestry on the floor, a strand of blonde hair on his pillow. She had left her mark everywhere.

Of the minutiae of the evening, Yoav remembered very little. But he did remember the sweep of sentiments. The urgency first, the humiliation second, and the affection last of all. Physically, he felt sick. But he also felt on a deeper level whole, as if the old gaping wound within him had been partly filled, if just a little bit by Liana Miller.

He smiled, thinking of her. And then the smile drooped as one particular memory came to mind. At the end of the night, he had asked her something. Something big. *Oh no*, he thought now. *What was it?!*

He stood up and began to pace back and forth. He was delirious with exhaustion and concern. What if he asked her something too big? What if he had scared her away? He tried to remember the words that had led up to that incoherent conversation.

"His name's Aaron," Yoav had said. "I'm worried about him."

"Does he love her?" she had asked.

Yoav remembered that part clearly. The repercussions of her question terrified him.

"I don't know," Aaron had responded. "But I have to go. He's my best friend."

Yoav recalled a minute or two of quiet passing between them. He could hardly bear this tension. In that shaded memory, what had transpired?

Then he remembered that she had answered, "Yes" to whatever it was he said. He frowned for a moment, looking at the blonde hair on his pillow, and then his eyebrows lifted. Yoav closed his eyes, exhaled with blissful relief and smiled. He remembered.

"Liana," he had asked her, "do you want to be my plus one?"

ACKNOWLEDGEMENTS

I want to thank first and foremost every member of my family.

My father taught me to love art. Together we watched foreign, silent and black and white films when I was a kid. He told me to look beyond the style and to appreciate the substance. Thank you, dad, for your influence and example.

I want to thank my mother for inspiring me with her love for literature. I will never forget how she read aloud The Lord of the Rings to me until I could read for myself. I thank you, mom, for those memories and for your patient guidance on this book.

To my three sisters, Dania, Leora and Dori, there are not enough words to express my gratitude and love for you each. Dania, you are my role model, the person I look up to and emulate most.

Leora, thank you for listening. Whether it was to a story I wrote or a true story I told, you were always there for me.

Dori, thank you for your friendship. There are few people whose opinions, convictions and loyalty I trust so deeply.

And to Conor and Noah, I thank you for never being strangers. You two are my brothers.

To my grandpa, David Iventosch, the most intelligent man I know, I thank you. Your determination to read each of my stories, your level criticisms and your incredibly generous support to fund the project, I can never repay. You are my hero, Papa.

There are too many friends to thank, but I must make a point in acknowledging two people. Will Newhart, my best friend, my male soulmate and meanest editor, this book would not be possible without you.

And to Shir Yehoshua, the girl who made me believe in my own worth and inspired me to self-publish this book. I owe you the world.

I must thank my editor Anna DeVries for her criticism and her encouraging words. And Luke Patterson for his elegant illustrations of the cover art.

To all the supporters of my Kickstarter campaign, who were so generous to donate to this project, I thank you.

In loving memory of Jack Colker. Dvorah Colker and family, the Fishbein family, Gary and Orna Lubliner, Jazz, Alex, Guy and Jacques Lubliner, Kirk and Sandi Iventosch, Leonard and Susie Iventosch, the Callison family, Isaac Negrin, Julie and Roni Ovadia, Lori Iventosch-James and Fred James, Barney Sherman, Gary Sherne and Sandy Frucht, Karla and Neil Smith, Arielle Beniacar, Patricia Newhart, the Shepherd family, Jo Alice and Wayne Canterbury, Bari Winchell, John and Marlene Falco, Kimberly Callison, Marissa Glidden, Ayala and Sam Mendelson, Riva Gambert and Sam Pitluck, Mike Fishbein, Gary Goldman, Hilary Balfour, Charles Sivakumaran, Amir Maltzman, David and Debby Shahvar, Kayla Robbins, Jeanette Bicais, Nathan Kaufman, Megan Pease, Jules LaCour, Yael Sherne, Zoe Wilson, Yair Muschinsky, Wendy Gordon, Anna Goldberg, Barbara Mutnick, Nitzhia Shaked, Yardena and Irv Brooks, Tsila and Nachum Schneidermann, Myrna and Rick Kimmelman, Eitan and Kim Davora, Marily Schnonthal, Shaani Applebaum, Sheldon Kahn, Stacey Costello, Dino Petrocco, Kevin Haggerty, Nina LaCour, Jacob Breall, Stacy Judson, Monica Butler, Larry and Ronnie Wanetick, Tzvi Sklar, Nilly Keren-Paz, Andrew Belinfante, Fraser Simons, Debby and Bill Kasson, Josh Weil, Courtney Fong, Nicolas Foucher, Kara Cobb, Steve Shafran, Aaron Levin, Lilit Marcus, Jonathan Glidden, Megan Caldwell, Gavin Schlissel,

ACKNOWLEDGEMENTS

Joe Morbin, Ryan Lee, Rachel Taketa, Loren Berman, Mark Patterson, Joseph D. Robbins, Brandon Kanechika, David Goldman, Jack Martin, Max Lavicka, Ysabel Goldberg, Jacques Lubliner, Gidon Gerstler, Nancy Carl, Samuel Burrell, Robin Siminovsky, Hilary Katersky, Amy Suto, Sarah Schmitt, Steph Scott, Michael Schonthal, Keren Brooks, Andy Lindquist, Anna Meyer, Moshe Radian, Laura Ferrante, Tali Azenkot, Caroline Keller-Lynn, Jessica Cooper, Austin Kilgore, Brett Edwards, Alexander Wold, Allison Siminovsky, Case Wiseman, Leon Blankrot, Evan Steele, Danielle Fallon, Nicola Griffith and Thorne Bird.

You each helped me achieve my dream and for that, I am forever grateful. This book is as much yours as it is mine.

GLOSSARY

A

Adei Ad – (Hebrew: עדי עד [ad-ey od] *lit.* For Always) An Israeli settlement in the West Bank, located near Shvut Rachel, another settlement.

Afula – A city in the North District of Israel.

Aliyah – (Hebrew: עלייה [aw-lee-yaw] *lit:* Ascent) The Immigration of Jews to the land of Israel. It is a basic tenet of Zionist ideology.

Amalek (ites) – (Hebrew: עמלק [am-*uh*-lyek] *lit:* Various Arabic and Hebrew Origins) A figure and nation in the Hebrew Bible, infamous for the unprovoked attack on the Israelites after their escape from Egypt (Deuteronomy, 25). King Saul is ordered by God to annihilate the entire race of Amalekites, including women, children and even livestock (Samuel, 15:17-8). His failure is considered, by folk tradition, the reason for the centurial resurrection of Amalek. Hamen (the Arch Villain in the Book of Purim), Hitler's Nazis and, even the Palestinians (as labeled by Jewish fundamentalists) are branded the modern reincarnations of this ancient evil. Furthermore, three out of the 613 Commandments are dedicated to remembering and exterminating Amalek.

Ani – (Hebrew: אני [ah-nee] *lit:* I)

Arak – (Arabic: ق رع [ar-*uh*k] *lit:* Sweet) An alcoholic spirit from the anis drinks family. It is a clear, colorless licorice-flavored distilled drink, popular in the Middle East.

Ars(im) – (Arabic: صرع [ahrs] *lit:* Pimp) A derogatory Hebrew slang term for the Israeli stereotype of a low-class young man. The Ars subculture is traditionally associated with the Jewish youth of Moroccan, Yemeni and Iranian origin.

Ashkenazi – (Hebrew: אשכנזי [osh-k*uh*-naz-ee] *lit:* Ashkenaz, Son of Gomer (Genesis 10)) A Jew descended from medieval communities along the Rhine in Germany, though modern usage encompasses most Eastern European Jewry. In Israel, the stigma supposes that Ashkenazi people are white, bland and/or pretentious.

B

Bachyan – (Hebrew: בכיין [baKH-yawn] *lit:* To Cry) A Hebrew slang term for cry-baby.

Baharat – (Arabic: بتاراهب [baw-hah-rot] *lit:* Spice) A spice mixture used in Arab cuisine most often to season meats and soups.

Beaufort – (French: Beau Fort [boo-fawr] *lit:* Beautiful Fortress) A crusader fortress in Southern Lebanon, occupied by Israel from 1982-2000, during the First Lebanese War.

Bedouin – (Arabic: نوّيودَب [bed-oo-in] *lit:* Those in the Desert) A predominately desert-dwelling Arabian ethnic group, divided into tribes and clans across the Middle East.

Beit Knesset – (Hebrew: בית כנסת [beyt k-nes-et] *lit:* House of Assembly)
A synagogue.

Bereishit – (Hebrew: בראשית [bur-ey-sheet] *lit:* In the Beginning) The
first book of the Hebrew Bible, also known as Genesis.

Bezalel – (Hebrew: בצלאל [bet-sawl-el] *lit:* In the Shadow of God) The
chief artisan of the tabernacle, his name adorns modern schools of art in
Israel and street signs, most prominently in Jerusalem.

Birthright – A non-profit educational organization that sponsors free heritage trips to Israel for young Jewish adults, most often college students,
who have never been to Israel.

Bissli – (Hebrew: ביסלי [bee-slee] *lit:* Bite For Me) An Israeli wheat snack
food that comes in an assortment of flavors.

Bizayon – (Hebrew: בזיון [biz-ahy-ohn] *lit:* Contempt, Shame) Disgrace.

C

Choze Lublin – (Hebrew: הזוה לובלין [KH-oh-zey loo-bleen] *lit:* The Seer
of Lublin) A Hasidic Rabbi from the city of Lublin, Poland. He became
known as the Seer due to his great intuitive powers.

Chutzpah – (Yiddish: חוצפה [KH-oot-sp*uh*] *lit:* Nerve, Insolence) A qual-
ity of audacity, for good or bad.

Coccinelle(im) – (French [kohk-see-nel] *lit:* Lady Bird) Based off the French
transsexual actress and entertainer of the early sixties (Jacques Charles Dufresnoy)

who called herself Coccinelle, the word is used in derogatory fashion in Israel. It is a common slur for transsexuals, transvestites, and homosexuals alike.

Confinement Base 394 – Also known as Prison Four, it is the main military prison for Israeli soldiers, located in a military police compound in Tzrifin.

D

Damon Runyon – An American newspaperman and author, best known for his short stories. He spun humorous tales of gamblers, hustlers, actors and gangsters. He wrote in so distinctive a vernacular style, that it was coined: Runyonese. His world is best known to the public by the musical "Guys and Dolls," based on two of his stories.

Dati(im) – (Hebrew: דתי [daw-tee] *lit:* Believer) A religious man, traditionally referring to one of Jewish faith.

Dizengoff – (Hebrew: דיזנגוף [dee-zen-gawf] *lit:* Meir Dizengoff, the First Mayor of Tel Aviv) One of the largest streets in Tel Aviv.

Djinn – (Arabic: جن [jeyn] *lit:* Hidden) Supernatural creatures, smokeless flames, or desert devils derived from the Qur'an and Arab folklore.

Duma – (Arabic: دوما [doo-m*uh*]) A Palestinian town in the Nablus Governorate of the Northern West Bank.

E

Endor – (Hebrew: אנדור [end-awr] *lit:* unknown) A Canaanite city first mentioned in the Book of Joshua. There, King Saul consulted the Witch of Endor to summon the spirit of the dead prophet Samuel the evening before the Battle of Gilboa in which he committed suicide. (Samuel 28:4-25) See: Saul.

G

Gaza Strip – On the Eastern Coast of the Mediterranean Sea, bordering Egypt on the southwest and Israel on the East and North. The land was occupied by Israel until the disengagement in 2005. Currently, governed by Hamas. See: Hamas.

Gilad Shalit – An Israeli soldier who was abducted inside Israel by Hamas militants in a cross-border raid near the Israeli border with Gaza in June 2006. Hamas held him for over five years until his release in October 2011 as part of a prisoner exchange deal. 1,027 Palestinian prisoners were given in return. See: Hamas.

Golda Meir – The Fourth Prime Minister of Israel and first woman to hold the position.

Golem – (Hebrew: גולם [goh-luhm] *lit:* Unshaped Form) In Jewish folklore, the Golem is an animated monster, created entirely from inanimate matter. The most famous narrative involves Judah Loew ben Bezalel, the late 16th century Rabbi of Prague, who brought the Golem to life to protect the city's Jews.

Goy(im) – (Hebrew: גוי [goi] *lit:* Nation) Gentile or non-Jew, derived from the Yiddish meaning.

H

Halacha – (Hebrew: הלכה [hah-*luh*-KHah] *lit:* To Walk, Go) The collective body of religious laws for Jews, including Biblical law (613 commandments) and later Talmudic and Rabbinic law.

Halamish – (Hebrew: חלמיש [KHah-*luh*-meesh] *lit:* Flint) A large communal Israeli settlement in the West Bank, located in the southwestern Samarian hills.

Hamas – (Arabic: حماس [KHah-maws] *lit:* Enthusiasm) The Palestinian Sunni Islamic political party that governs the Gaza Strip, defined by the European Union, the United States, Israel and other countries as a terrorist organization.

Hannah Senesh – One of thirty-seven Jews from Mandatory Palestine parachuted by the British army into Yugoslavia during World War II to assist the rescue of Hungarian Jews about to be deported to Death Camp Auschwitz. She was captured, tortured and executed by a German firing squad. She is regarded as a national hero in Israel.

Har Dov – (Hebrew: הר דוב [hahr *duhv*] *lit:* Mountain named after Dov Rodberg, an IDF officer killed there in 1970) Also known as Shebba Farms, the territory is uninhabited strip of land claimed by Lebanon, however conquered in 1967 by Israel from Syria. The United Nations recognizes this land as belonging to Syria. The surrounding borders are heavily fortified by both the IDF and Hezbollah.

Haredi(im) – (Hebrew: חרדים [KHah-rey-dee] *lit:* Fear, Anxiety) An intensely conservative Orthodox Jew, most often referred to as an Ultra-Orthodox. The name is derived from God-fearing.

Harem – (Arabic: حرم [hair-*uh*m] *lit:* Forbidden, Sacred) A household made up solely of women, originating in the Near East an Ottoman empire. Depictions in contemporary Western culture illustrate a lustful side to the harem, almost indicative of a brothel.

Har Herzel – (Hebrew: הר הרצל [hahr her-ts*uh*l] *lit:* Mount of Herzl) Also known as the Mount of Rememberance, Har Herzl is Israel's national cemetery, found on the west side of Jerusalem. It is named for the founder of modern Zionism, Theodor Herzl. See: Theodor Herzl.

Hasmonean – (Hebrew: חשמונאי [haz-m*uh*-nee-u*hn*] *lit:* Josephus Flavius) The ruling dynasty of Judea and surrounding regions during classical antiquity. Starting with Simon Maccabeus, brother of Judah the Maccabee, the "hammer" hero of the revolt against the Selucid army.

Ha'aretz – (Hebrew: הארץ [hah-ahr-ets] *lit:* Land) Another name for Israel, meaning the Land.

Hezbollah – (Arabic: حزب الله [KHes-bah-lah] *lit:* Party of God) A Shi'a militant group and political party based in Lebanon. Initiated during the Lebanese Civil War in 1982, Hezbollah was Israel's main opponent in the Second Lebanon War. Hezbollah receives military training, weapons and financial support from Iran and political support from Syria.

Highway 90 – The world's lowest road and Israel's longest road, this Israeli highway stretches from the Lebanese Border until the southern border with Egypt.

Highway 443 – A divided four-lane route connecting the West Bank to Israel. Although Palestinians have a legal right to use the route, they often refer to it is as the "Apartheid Road" due its problematic location and history of limiting Palestinian traffic as a response to the violence of the Second Intifadah.

Hillel – Also known as Hillel: The Foundation for Jewish Campus Life is the largest Jewish organization on college campuses in the world.

Holy of Holies – (Hebrew: קודש הקודשים *lit:* Most Holy Place) A term in the Hebrew Bible which refers to the inner sanctuary of the Tabernacle and later the Temple of Jerusalem where the Arc of the Covenant was kept.

Hookah – (Sanscrit: नारकेला [*hook-uh*] *lit:* Coconut) A single or multi-stemmed waterpipe, an instrument for smoking flavored tobacco, originating in India and Persia and popular to this day all across Asia and Africa.

Humash – (Hebrew: חומש [KH*oo*-mosh] *lit:* The Hebrew Bible in printed form (as opposed to the scroll).

J

Jacob – (Hebrew: יעקב *lit:* Leg-puller) The third patriarch of the Hebrew people with whom God made a covenant and ancestor of the Tribes of

Israel, which were named after his descendants, according to the Hebrew Bible.

Jalud – (Arabic: جَالُود [jaw-lood]) A Palestinian village in the Nablus Governorate of the Northern West Bank, northeast of Shilo.

Jericho – (Hebrew: יריחו [jer-i-koh] *lit:* Moon) Described in the Hebrew Bible as the "City of Palm Trees," Jericho's walls fell at the sound of the Israelite army's horns. (Joshua, 6:1-27)

Jobnik – (English/Yiddish: Job/Nik) An Israeli slang term for a non-combat Israeli soldier, often tinged with insult or contempt.

Job – (Hebrew: איוב [job] *lit:* Hated) The central character of the Book of Job in the Hebrew Bible. Job is a blessed righteous man who slowly loses everything and yet remains faithful. This, as a result of Satan's challenge to God to test the integrity of Job's faith.

Jonah – (Hebrew: יונה [joh-n*uh*] *lit:* Dove) A prophet of the Northern kingdom of Israel, famous for being swallowed whole by a whale in his fruitless attempts to evade God (Book of Jonah).

Judea – (Hebrew: יהודה [joo-dee-*uh*] *lit:* Kingdom of Judah) The mountainous southern part of Israel, named for the Kingdom. Judea and Samaria are what Israelis, particularly religious Jews, refer to as the West Bank.

K

Kaddish – (Hebrew: קדיש [kah-dish] *lit:* Holy) A prayer found in the Jewish prayer service, dedicated to the magnification and sanctification of

God's name. The term is often used to refer specifically to the Mourner's Kaddish, as part of Jewish mourning rituals.

Kalash (Russian: Кала́шников [kah-lawsh] *lit:* Mikhael Kalashnikov) – An Israeli military slang term for an AK-47, the rifle most often carried by Hamas and Hezbollah insurgents.

Kanai(im) – (Hebrew: קנאי [kah-nahy-ee] *lit:* Zealot) One who is zealous on behalf of God. In biblical texts, the term is often implied as a great compliment (see: Pinhas).

Keffiyeh – (Arabic: كوفية [*kuh-fee-uh*] *lit:* Unknown) A traditional Arab headdress fashioned from a square, usually cotton scarf. For Palestinians, the black and white Keffiyeh is a nationalistic symbol, made most famous by Yasser Arafat, President of the Palestinian Liberation Organization.

Kibbutz(im) – (Hebrew: קיבוץ [kee-boots] *lit:* Gathering, Clustering) A collective "utopian" community, combining tenets of Zionism and socialism, in Israel. Although, traditionally based on agriculture, the modern Kibbutz includes industrial plants, high-tech enterprises, and immigrant absorption centers.

Kohav HaShahar – (Hebrew: כוכב השחר [koh-KH*uhv* hah-shah-KHahr] *lit:* Morning Star) An Israeli settlement in the Binyamin region of the Northern West Bank.

Konenut – (Hebrew: כוננות [kohn-en-oot] *lit:* Preparedness, Readiness) Literally defined as vigilance and preparedness, but in military jargon, also referring to ammunition and equipment. This link comes from the consistent need to be "vigilant" and check that the cartridges and equipment are all full and prepared for combat.

Korah – (Hebrew: קרח [kohr-aKH] *lit:* Baldness, Ice) Leading a small revolt against Moses, God punishes Korah and his supporters by burning and burying them alive. (Numbers 16:1-40)

Krav Maga – (Hebrew: קרב מגע [k-rahv mah-guh] *lit:* Contact Combat) A non-competitive martial art and eclectic self-defense system developed in Israel that involves striking techniques, wrestling and grappling.

Kus'emek – (Arabic: كمأ سك. [*koo*s ehm-ek] *lit:* Your Mother's Vagina) A popular Arabic and Hebrew expletive meant to curse the moment someone is born, literally cursing the vagina from which the person came forth.

L

Lilith – (Hebrew: לילית [lil-ith] *lit:* Night) First defined as a female demon (Isaiah 34:14), Lilith is more famous in Jewish folklore as the first wife of Adam, made up, like him, of the Earth. Painted most often as a villain for refusing to be subservient to Adam (Alphabet of Ben Sira, Aggadish Midrashim, the Zohar).

Li'or – (Hebrew: ליאור [lee-awr] *lit:* My Light) A night vision scope, known as the Land Warrior PVS-14, applicable to M-4 and TAR 21 semi-automatic rifles among others.

Lochem – (Hebrew: לוחם [loh-KHem] *lit:* Warrior) Defined literally as Warrior, this is the appellation given by the IDF to every combat soldier.

Lone Soldier – (Hebrew: חייל בודד) The name given to a soldier in the IDF whose parents do not reside in Israel during his or her service. The Lone Soldier is an immigrant or a foreign volunteer, most often motivated by his or her Jewish heritage and an intense identification with Zionism.

M

M-16 – (English: Rifle, Caliber 5.56 mm, M16) The United States military designation for the AR-15 rifle adapted for semi-automatic, three-round burst and full-automatic fire. Until November 2009, the M-16 and M-4 were the standard infantry weapons for the Israeli military. The Israeli-made MTR-21 replaced the American rifle.

M-4 – (English: M-4 Carbine) A family of firearms tracing its lineage back to earlier carbine versions of the M-16 rifle. The M-4 is shorter and lighter variant of the M-16.

Malaki – (Arabic: مَلَكي [Muh-lah-kee] *lit:* Royal, Kingly) A lithological type of white, coarsely crystalline, thickly bedded limestone found in the Judean hills in Israel and the West Bank. Popularly referred to as Jerusalem Stone.

Malamnik – (Hebrew: משקיע למען המפקד [muh-lahm-nik] *lit:* Strives to Impress the Commander) An abbreviated Israeli military slang term for a brown-nose or ass-kisser.

Masa – (Hebrew: מסע [Muh-saw] *lit:* Journey) Literally defined as journey or voyage, the Masa in Israeli military lingo is known as the 40-50 kilometer hike every combat soldier must complete in his or her basic training in order to graduate. Traditionally, the Masa takes place in the Negev Desert and soldiers receive their unit's specialized beret upon completion.

Mefaked(im) – (Hebrew: מפקד [mi-faw-ked] *lit:* Commander)

Mem Mem – (Hebrew: מפקד מחלקה [mem mem] *lit:* Commander of the Platoon, Officer)

Mem Pay – (Hebrew: פלוגה מפקד [mem pey] *lit:* Commander of the Company, Captain)

Mike's Place – Established in 1992, the Israeli sports bar/restaurant has six locations, including two in Tel Aviv and is frequented most often by American and foreign crowds. The common language spoken there is English and the American-ized menu includes bacon, BBQ wings and chicken fingers.

Minyan – (Hebrew: מניין [meen-yuhn] *lit:* to count, number) The minimum of ten Jewish adults required for certain religious obligations, such as public prayer services.

Mitzvah(ot) – (Hebrew: מצווה [meets-vah] *lit:* Command) Defined literally as a divine commandment and moral law, there are 613 in the Hebrew Bible.

Misken – (Hebrew: מסכן [mees-ken] *lit:* Poor) A Hebrew slang term for "poor thing," often used as a sympathetic (or adversely, ironic) designation to another person's emotional state.

Mizrahi – (Hebrew: מזרחי [mees-rah-KHee] *lit:* Eastern) A Jew descended from the Jewish communities of the Middle East, North Africa and the Caucasus. The term Mizrahi is used in Israel for Jews from mostly Arab-ruled geographies and primarily Muslim-majority countries such as: Iraq, Syria, Lebanon, Yemen, Azerbaijan, Iran, and Afghanistan. Sephardi Jews from Morocco, Algeria or Turkey are erroneously grouped into the Mizrahi category.

Moshe Rabbeinu – (Hebrew: משה [moh-sheh rab-ahy-noo] *lit:* To Draw) Moses, a religious leader, law-giver and prophet to whom the authorship of the Hebrew Bible is traditionally attributed. The addition of "Rabbeinu" to his name, means "Our Teacher/Rabbi".

Moshiach – (Hebrew: משיח [moh-shee-ahKH] *lit:* Anointed One, Messiah) A term used in the Hebrew Bible to describe priests and kings, who were traditionally anointed with holy anointing oil (Exodus, 30:22-25). Traditional and current Orthodox thought have held that the Messiah will be "the anointed one," a descendant of the Davidic line, who will gather the Jews back into the Land of Israel, usher in the era of peace and rebuild the Third Temple. Furthermore, Ultra-Orthodox Jews do not accept the legitimacy of the State of Israel, contesting that no true Jewish state will exist until the Moshiach's return.

Mount Hermon – (Hebrew: הר חרמון [KHuhr-mohn] *lit:* Mountain of the Chief) A mountain cluster, bordering Lebanon, Syria and Israel. On top is the buffer zone between Syria and Israel, the highest manned U.N. position in the world.

Mount Nebo – (Hebrew: הר נבו [nee-boh]) Mount Nebo is where the Hebrew prophet Moses looked unto the Promised Land and where he died (Deuteronomy, 34:1).

Musakhan – (Arabic: مُسَخَّن [moo-saw-kahn]) A traditional Palestinian dish, composed of taboon bread baked with pine nuts, onions, spices and often roasted chicken.

N

Nahlaot – (Hebrew: נחלאות [nah-KH-law-oht]) A cluster of neighborhoods in Central Jerusalem, known for its narrow winding lanes, old-style housing, hidden courtyards and many small synagogues.

Nahliel – (Hebrew: נחליאל [nah-KH-lee-el]) A small, isolated settlement in the West Bank established in 1984 by Ultra-Orthodox Jews.

Nakpadon – (Hebrew: נקפדון [nok-puh-dohn]) An Armored Personnel Carrier (APC) is an armored fighting vehicle designed to transport infantry to the battlefield.

Naot – (Hebrew: נאות [naw-oht] *lit:* Proper) A leather sandal from the Israeli shoe company Teva Naot, similar in shape and style to the Birkenstock brand.

Nu – (Yiddish: נו [noo] *lit:* Unknown) A multi-purpose interjection often analogous to "well?" or "so?" suggesting impatience.

O

Oketz – (Hebrew: עוקץ [oh-kets] *lit:* Sting) Although literally defined as "sting," in Israeli army slang it means a soldier who cheats his or her way out of work.

Outpost – A Jewish community built within the West Bank (Judea and Samaria) after 1991 without the authorization of the Israeli government.

P

Payot – (Hebrew: פאות [pey-oht] *lit:* Corner) Sidelocks or sidecurls worn by some men in the Orthodox Jewish community based on a biblical command against shaving the corners of one's head.

Philistine – (Hebrew: פלשתי [fil-*uh*-steen] *lit:* To Divide, To Invade) A people who appeared in the southern coastal area of Canaan (modern day Gaza) at the beginning of the Iron Age (circa 1175 B.C.), most likely from the Aegean region. The Hebrew Bible paints them as the Kingdom of Israel's most dangerous enemy.

Pinhas – (Hebrew: פנחס [peen-KHaws] *lit:* Bronze-Colored One) A High Priest of Israel in the wilderness who distinguishes himself as a youth by his zeal (Numbers 25:1-9). As the Moabite and Midianite tribes tempt the Israelites to worship idols, Pinhas personally executes an Israelite man and Mideanite woman lying together in the man's tent. Pinhas is commended for preventing Israel's fall to idolatrous practices. See: Kana'i.

Pikuach Nefesh – (Hebrew: פיקוח נפש [peek-*oo*-aKH neh-fesh] *lit:* Saving a Life) The principle in Jewish Law, stating that the preservation of human life overrides any other religious consideration.

R

Rebbe – (Yiddish: רבי [reb-*uh*] *lit:* My Master, Teacher) Derived from the Hebrew word for Rabbi, the Rebbe is the leader and teacher of the Jewish community.

S

Samaria – See: Judea

Saul – (Hebrew: שאול [sawl] *lit:* Asked For, Prayed For) The first king of the United Kingdom of Israel, anointed by the prophet Samuel, kills himself in the Battle of Gilboa to avoid capture.

Settlement – A Jewish civilian community built on land that was captured by Israel from Jordan, Egypt or Syria during the 1967 Six-Day War. Settlements exist in the West Bank, East Jerusalem and the Golan Heights (all settlements in the Sinai and the Gaza Strip were disengaged in 1982 and 2005, respectively). Israel continues to expand its settlements and settle new areas in the West Bank in spite of the Oslo Accords that barred both Israelis and Palestinians from any unilateral undertaking that would alter the status quo. The international community considers the settlements in occupied territory to be illegal, while Israel disputes the legal arguments that were used to declare the settlements illegal.

Shabbat – (Hebrew: שבת [shah-baht] *lit:* Rest, Cessation) The seventh day of the Jewish Week, known as the day of rest; the Sabbath.

Shawarma – (Arabic: الشاورما [shaw-wawr-m*uh*] *lit:* Turning) A Levantine meat preparation where lamb, goat, chicken, turkey, beef or mixed meats are placed on a spit and may be grilled for as long as a day.

Shebba Farms – See: Har Dov

Shekel – (Akkadian: **šiqlu** [shek-*uh*l] *lit:* Weighing) The Shekel is any of several ancient units of weight or of currency. The first usage is from Mesopotamia around 3000 B.C. The current Israeli currency is the Shekel.

Shilo – (Hebrew: שילה [shee-loh]) An ancient city south of ancient Tirzah and mentioned in the Hebrew Bible. It was the temporary capital of Israel before the first Temple was built in Jerusalem.

Shuk – (Arabic: قوس [sh*oo*k]) An open-air marketplace, traditionally in an Arab city.

Shvut Rachel – (Hebrew: שבות רחל [sh-voot rah-KHel]) An Israeli settlement and city in the West Bank, located 45 kilometers North of Jerusalem, located in the Shilo area in Binyamin.

Siddur – (Hebrew: סידור [see-duhr] *lit:* Arrangement) A Jewish prayer book, containing a set order of daily prayers.

Sideways – A hole-in-the-wall bar located in central Jerusalem.

Sikrikim – (Latin: Siccari [seek-reek-eem] *lit:* Daggers) A group of Ultra-Orthodox virulently anti-Israel Jews who gained international attention for acts of violence committed against Orthodox Jewish institutions and individuals who would not comply with their extremist demands. Their name is an allusion of to the Jewish zealots who attacked Jews and Romans alike during the Roman conquest of Judea, concealing daggers, *sicae* in Latin.

Slicha – (Hebrew: סליחה [slee-KH*uh*] *lit:* Excuse Me, Pardon, Sorry)

Solomon – (Hebrew: שלמה [sol-*uh*-m*uh*n] *lit:* Peaceful) The third King of the United Kingdom of Israel, the builder of the First Temple in Jerusalem, the wise poet, philanderer and man of countless legends in Jewish folklore.

Sylvester – (Latin: Sivla [sil-ves-ter] *lit:* Wood, Forest) The Catholic name for the New Year's celebration, named after the Roman Pope and Saint, Sylvester I, who convinced Constantine to ban Jews from living in the city of Jerusalem (325 A.D.). His Saint's day is December 31st and thus the New Year is dedicated to his memory. In Israel, the Catholic name is used simply because the Jewish New Year takes precedence, following the lunar calendar.

T

Teffillin – (Hebrew: תפילין [tuh-fee-leen] *lit:* To Guard, Protect) A small set of black leather boxes containing scrolls of parchment, inscribed with verses of the Hebrew Bible, which are worn by observant Jews during weekday morning prayers.

The Blue Line – A border demarcation between Lebanon and Israel published by the United Nations in June 2000 for the purposes of determining whether Israel had fully withdrawn from Lebanon.

Theodor Herzl – A Jewish Austro-Hungarian journalist and the father of modern political Zionism and in effect the state of Israel. See: Zionism.

Throbe – (Arabic: ثَوب [throhb] *lit:* Garment) An ankle-length garment, usually with long sleeves, similar to a robe, commonly worn in Arab countries.

Torah – (Hebrew: תורה [tor-ruh] *lit:* Instruction, Teaching) The Jewish name for the first five books of the Hebrew Bible.

Tzair (im) – (Hebrew: צעיר [tsahy-eer] *lit:* Young) Literally defined as young, in Israeli military slang, the word means a newly enlisted soldier, a tenderfoot.

Tzav Rishon – (Hebrew: צו ראשון [tsahv ree-shohn] *lit:* First Order) The first call to all Israeli citizens to enlist in the military. At the age of 16-17, most Israeli youth report to the induction centers.

W

West Bank – The West Bank of the Jordan River is the landlocked geographical area that shares its northern, western and southern borders with Israel. Since the 1993 Oslo Accords, parts of the West Bank are under full control of the Palestinian Authority.

Y

Yehoshua (Joshua) – (Hebrew: יהושע [ye-hoh-shoo-uh] *lit:* God is Salvation) First, a spy, then the assistant of Moses, Joshua becomes the leader of the Israelites after Moses' death.

Yeshiva – (Hebrew: ישיבה [ye-shee-v*uh*] *lit:* Sitting) A Jewish educational institution that focuses on the study of traditional religious texts.

Yiddish – A high German language of Ashkenazi Jewish origin. Written in the Hebrew alphabet, the language is a fusion of Hebrew and Aramaic into German dialects.

Yonatan Netanyahu – A commander of an elite Israeli commando unit, he was the only soldier to die in the daring Operation Entebbe in Uganda. Considered a hero in Israel, his brother Benjamin (Bibi) Netanyahu is the current Prime Minister.

Z

Zionism – A form of nationalism of Jews and Jewish culture that supports a Jewish nation state in territory defined as the Land of Israel.

Ilan Benjamin

Ilan Benjamin served in a combat unit in the Israel Defense Forces from November 2009 to May 2012. He self-published his first book *Masa: Stories of a Lone Soldier* in November 2012. He currently studies Screen Writing at the University of Southern California.

Made in the USA
Charleston, SC
07 December 2012